My Amish Rose

Quilted Hills, Volume 4

Piper Forrest and Lily Simmons

Published by Bev Haynes, 2021.

MY AMISH ROSE

First edition. May 1, 2021.

ISBN: 979-8201879174

Written by Piper Forrest and Lily Simmons.

Table of Contents

Dear Reader,

We hope you'll enjoy getting to know the people of Paradise Wells. The adventures are just beginning, so if you'd like to follow along, we invite you to visit our blog, where you'll receive special notifications as new books in this series are released. We also hope you'll consider dropping a quick review at the retailer of your choice. Thank you, and happy reading!

Piper and Lily

Prologue

T*hen...*

Iris pushed open the heavy, leaded-glass door. Streaks of red and orange filled the evening sky. She overstayed her time at the library and *daed* wouldn't be happy with her. She had chores to do before supper.

The thrill of completing the testing for her General Educational Development diploma, GED, paled as she rushed through the doors and skipped down the steps. Iris wrapped a sweater tightly around her body as there was a breeze. In the Spring, evenings could be chilly.

She only told her friend, Caleb, about completing her education. As of last night, he was more than her friend. He was her fiancée. He asked her to marry him after the singing at the Bishop's home.

Her parents wouldn't understand why a newly engaged girl would have any higher education desires, but Iris loved learning. Sadness overwhelmed her when her education ended in the Spring of eighth grade. Caleb understood, though. He felt proud to know her final test was underway this afternoon.

Her mother had invited Caleb to supper tonight, and Iris could hardly wait until after the meal. She and Caleb planned to tell her parents about the engagement. Afterward, they would go to his parents and tell them as well.

If she weren't eighteen, she would skip down the street to where she tied her horse and buggy, but a child-like giggle burst through her lips instead. As she began to untie the leather straps from the hitching post, she felt a creepy sensation skitter up her spine. Then someone grabbed her from behind. She couldn't see who it was, but she smelled cigarette smoke and stale sweat.

Iris twisted her body and tried to bite his arm, but she failed to reach it. Before she could scream, his other hand covered her mouth.

Gott help me! When she thought it could not get worse, another man showed up. This one wore a knitted ski mask. He bent forward and grabbed her legs. She was helpless as they rushed her off behind the library parking lot and behind a giant steel dumpster.

Later, when they were finished with her and ran off into a thick grove of trees, she lay on the cold asphalt and cried. They raped her and laughed at their success in taking a virginal Amish girl. But the joke was on them, were the only words of comfort she could give herself. Last night after accepting Caleb's proposal, her virginity ended.

Panic filled her. She couldn't go home looking like this. She felt bruising must show around her throat, and when she succeeded in biting one of them, they slapped her hard across the face. Daed wouldn't care whether he was Amish or Englisch. He would track these men down and possibly beat them to a pulp.

Iris shook her head to clear her mind. She'd have to wait until her parents went to bed before she could slip into the house. Gathering the ripped material around her, she searched for the straight pins she used to close the front of her dress every day. She found two pins, then did her best to cover herself. The sweater helped a lot and added a bit of warmth, but her whole body trembled.

She had to get out of here before someone found her this way. The humiliation would be too great. She'd never tell Caleb nor her family what happened. How would she explain to them why she missed supper? Iris had been so happy an hour ago, but now? After being thrust into madness, she didn't know what to do.

It was dark where she'd tethered the horse, so Iris made her way to the rig and climbed onto the seat. It was easy releasing the horse in the dark as she'd done it so many times. Her only plan was to get the horse and buggy home, then hide until everyone in the house went to bed. Then she'd sneak in and go to her room. Hopefully, no one would catch her. Her mind and body were both numb. She tried to pray, but the words failed to come from her heart to her heavenly father. This numbness was the worst of all.

Caleb and Mr. King looked at each other. He saw the worry in the man's eyes. The man looked away, trying to hide his fear from him, but it worried Caleb sick. Where was Iris?

"Don't worry so much about her, Caleb," the older man said, "Iris is still on *rumspringa*, for sure and for certain. She probably went to one of her friends' homes and lost track of time. It's not unusual for her."

Caleb bit his lip. Who was Micah trying to convince Caleb or himself?

"*Jah*, eat your supper. You can come back and see her tomorrow," Naomi King said to him, care and understanding shown from her eyes. "One thing you need to know about our Iris, she is very independent."

Caleb nodded as if he understood, but he didn't. He hurried to finish supper so he could go out and find her. "I will get her and bring her home." His voice shook, and his middle pulled with dread.

Looking around the kitchen, Caleb saw the battery lamps were on because complete darkness descended. The rich chicken and noodle dinner, once appetizing, now made his stomach churn, giving him a nauseous feeling. "Thank you for supper, but I cannot stay any longer. I'm off to look for Iris."

Micah King nodded. "If you're out looking for her, we will stay here and wait for her return. She will most probably be back while you are away scouring the town for her." A chuckle followed his words. "We'll see you tomorrow, son."

Caleb took his coat from a peg at the back door of the mud room, then he flew out the door and rushed to his rig of one horse and a covered buggy. He must find Iris. Deep fear pulled at him. Where was she?

It was late when Iris brought the horse and buggy into the barn. She had no intention of brushing the horse. Instead, leading him to his stall and making sure he had hay and water. The only thing she could think to do was wait and make sure everyone was asleep, then sneak into the house.

The cold night air seeped into the barn, and Iris could wait no longer to get inside to the warmth of the house. It was late enough to go in without someone seeing her.

Slipping from the barn, she raced across the area covered in short grass to the house. Quietly, she opened the back door and went in. She nearly made it to the stairs.

"Iris, come here. I want to speak to you."

The shock of *daed*'s words startled her. The only light came from the glow of the stove. Hopefully, *daed* wouldn't see her disheveled appearance. Taking a deep breath, she moved closer.

"Where have you been? All of us have been worried about you. Caleb was here, you know. He went out to look for you."

"I-I, don't know what to say. I stayed at the library too long."

"What's the matter with you? You look upset. And your dress and *kapp* are askew."

"N-Nothing. It's late, and I should go to bed." Iris turned, to go but her *daed* spoke before she got far.

"Stop." His voice was loud and firm. "I want you to know I saw you and Caleb in the barn Sunday night. I was not going to say a thing, but now, I have to. It looks like Caleb found you, and you two had it out. You are hurt."

Iris couldn't find the words to answer him. Instead, she began to sob. "No!" She then rushed to the stairs.

"Tomorrow, I'm contacting the Bishop about this." He stepped toward the stairs, where she stopped when he spoke. "We will deal with Caleb. You are never to have another thing to do with that man, do you understand?"

Instead of answering, Iris raced up the stairs to her room.

Iris packed the few English garments she hid in her trunk at the end of the bed. She had two sets she could wear when she and her friend Emma Werner traveled into the town to meet friends at a movie.

Dressed warmly in her jeans and sweatshirt, Iris quietly slipped down the stairs and through the dark kitchen. She dropped a note on the table, then made her way to the mudroom for her heavy coat. With all that happened, she couldn't live here anymore.

Salty tears rolled down her cheeks. She would miss her brothers and her parents, but more than the family, she'd miss Caleb the most.

She opened the door and stepped into a life so unfamiliar and frightening. Forgive me, *Gott*, she whispered, then closed the door on her life as she knew it.

Chapter One

Now...

Iris stepped from the bus at Paradise Wells after a two-hour trip from Lancaster, Pennsylvania, where she lived for six years. If her car hadn't been in the shop, the journey would have taken less than an hour. The bus stopped at every small town along the way and at every convenience store gas station for pit stops.

Stepping to the side to let others off the bus, she filled her lungs with the sweet smell of home, but all she took in were the fetidness of diesel fumes and cigarette smoke. Over the years, she missed this town. When she was younger, she thought it was a huge place, but looking at it today, after the years away from Paradise Wells, living in Lancaster, she realized it was a small place, not over five thousand people. She'd built-up in her mind how arriving back home would be, but it was nothing like her dreams.

The bus driver slung her duffle bag from the coach and nearly crawled inside to reach other passengers' belongings. Iris bent, grasped the retractable handle, set the bag upright, and pulled it into the terminal. Each time the plastic wheels rolled over a seam in the large vinyl tiles, they made a clattering sound.

People stood in line by the vending machines where cold sandwiches enticed the hungry to part with money they could ill afford to spend. A dozen or more children bounced in front of the parents, irritating their mothers as they cried for sweets. Searching the walls, she found the bulletin board crammed full of a variety of ads. Scanning momentarily, she found it. Eddie Vogel's number. He still ran his shuttle service for the Amish community. Pulling her cell from her back pocket, she dialed him. The phone rang once.

"Hello?" A man answered.

"I'm calling for a ride from the bus station in Paradise Wells."

"Name, please?" His response was brusque. Iris attended school with his children. The man talked gruff, to be sure, and he was a busy body as well.

She hesitated. Could she cope with the community discovering that she came to visit her family? It was too late for worry. She had to follow through with her impulsive decision. The reason she returned home was too important to worry about the district and how they felt about her.

When she gave Eddie Vogel her name, she felt sure everyone he saw for the rest of the day would hear from him that she returned. "This is Iris. Iris King."

There was a pause, and then a snort came over the line. "Well, well. The black sheep has returned."

Iris closed her eyes, trying to reach a calm place before she spoke a word. She didn't have to wait long. Eddie asked, "So you want a ride out to your parents' house?"

"Yes." The word tangled in her mind before bursting out sharply.

"I'll be there in less than five minutes. I'm already in town. Just wait out front for me."

She thanked him and walked to the front of the building where the automatic glass door, covered by a roof, held back the thin, autumn sun. As she neared, it slid open for her to exit the building. People stood underneath the entrance, waiting for rides. The roof overhang captured cigarette fumes from several young people, causing a thick haze. It made her feel like coughing. How could people continue the dangerous habit? Iris worried about how her lungs reacted to the secondhand smoke.

She looked up as Eddie arrived in a large, new vehicle. Was it a suburban? It held three or four rows of seats. It tipped her off that his business thrived since she'd been away.

Eddie took her bag and tossed it in the row behind her, and she entered the car, sliding into the passenger seat behind the driver. It was warm inside the luxurious interior. This November day turned cold, and two weeks from Thanksgiving, it brought back a squeezing sensitivity in her middle. Homesickness? She had little time to ponder her situation. She was here for a reason, and as much as it upset her, she had to be home to do it. Rose's life depended on the answers she received.

Iris' mother, Naomi, stood looking at her with round eyes, which filled with tears. "Iris? My beautiful daughter!" She threw her arms around Iris and held her in her full, pronounced bosom. *Maem* smelled the same as she remembered. An aroma of yeasty bread and the sweetness of apples. *Maem*'s was the scent of unconditional love.

She pulled out of her *maem*'s hug to look at her. Little had changed over the six, nearly seven years she was away. A narrowing of her blue eyes warned Iris of a problem lurking. Here was the first sign that she shouldn't have come here for help.

"*Maem*, is it alright that I'm here? Daed..."

"You are worried about what he will say, *Jah*?"

Difficulty in swallowing kept her from answering. Iris nearly burst into tears. Her parents had always helped her navigate troubling situations, and, boy, did she ever need them to do so, now. Iris nodded, dropped the bag, and her jacket by the front door, and followed her mother. How would her family regard her wearing jeans and an over-sized sweatshirt? She still wore her hair long and, in a braid, wrapped around the back of her head. Never accustomed to makeup, her face was bare.

"Come in. We are all in the kitchen for supper." *Maem* turned and strode to the kitchen doorway. "We are just finishing. Do you want something to eat? We have plenty."

Iris looked into the room. There were bowls with remains of stew in them. Fresh bread with real butter and a double-crusted pie stood on the pie safe near the window. The scene before her caused her to think of a snow globe. The same picture, the same snow. Little had changed.

Iris answered from behind her. "No, but thank you for the offer. My stomach is in knots of nerves."

Maem stopped and turned around to face her before they entered the kitchen. "Are you well, daughter? Are you here to stay?"

Iris shook her head and said, "I'm fine, but I only have one day to spend with you. Then I have to return to my work. I am a Nurse Practitioner, and I work in the emergency room at Lancaster General Hospital."

"You are a nurse?" *Maem* questioned. "That is important work." The expression on *maem*'s face dropped with sad disappointment that she wasn't staying permanently, then she quickly pulled herself together, turned, and strode into the kitchen and said, "Look who I found at the door!" *Maem* stepped to the side, and Iris came into full view of the rest of her family.

Daed still sat at the head of the table, and her two brothers on one side and a vacant spot on the other was *maem*'s place. Oh, how the boys had grown. Ben had been ten and Jacob twelve when she left. Now, they were nearly men at ages sixteen and eighteen.

"Iris!" They whooped in unison and jumped from their chairs, eager to reach her.

"Sit!" Her father hollered. She saw a cold, stern look cross his face. Her brothers returned to their chairs at his demand. He aged a little, but he was still a handsome man of forty-five. His hair showed a few grays, and they caught the light and glistened. "Why are you here? Haven't you caused us enough pain with your disappearance into the Englisch world?"

"Micah! Please..." Her mother said tersely.

Iris's breath caught in her chest, and she was unsure how to respond. She'd hoped *daed* would welcome her home, but she could see this was not the case. How could she ask for help when he acted like this? Would he pass judgment on her even though it was not the Amish way and forbidden by the *Ordnung*? A Bible verse popped into her mind. *Vengeance is mine, I will repay, says the Lord.*

Biting on her bottom lip, she carefully planned her words.

She must say it now, no backing down in fear. "I've come to see if you will help save your granddaughter's life."

CHAPTER TWO

Caleb Miller left the furniture shop behind his house and brushed the sawdust from his clothes. He worked on a dining room table today. With the two leaves added, it would seat sixteen people. Six on each side and two at each end. Something perfect for a large family.

He learned his craft at his father, David Miller's knee, got knowledge from his *daed* and daadi before him. The tradition went back four generations. Miller's Fine Furniture was now his. Caleb's father was ill with Parkinson's disease and could no longer use the tools to make furniture, but he was still a great help to him.

Recently Caleb opened a sales outlet in downtown Paradise Wells to showcase the beautiful work. His father quickly became a fixture at the store, greeting customers, showing them items they were interested in seeing. It meant a lot to his *daed* to have a purpose. It also gave his *maem* some freedom, as well. She enjoyed having her own space when everyone was away during working hours.

It was now five o'clock. Caleb and his helper, Jimmy, returned from an appointment with Angela James. She bought two toy chests, one each for her sons, for Christmas. They delivered the boxes at four-thirty when the woman came home from her job as a lawyer in the city. Happily, she'd ordered well before the holiday because he got many calls for Christmas gifts from the Englisch. Caleb's list grew so large, and he contemplated looking for new woodworkers to help him. The trouble was, he was picky about his work, and he wouldn't hire anyone who didn't have his high standards of quality artistry.

Caleb spoke to Marvin Thomas, a carpenter who owned a small furniture shop in the next community over. It had once been part of a much larger district where he lived, but the area expanded and separated into two residential sections. Marvin's residence was near the Miller home and shop. Caleb was determined to try one more time to give Marvin a job with a substantial increase in the offer. One with profit on the items he created. Caleb hoped the offer of higher wages and profit-sharing would keep Marvin's quality high and bring in the products' highest purchase prices.

Their community also had another carpenter. Micah King. His father told him how they worked together when they were younger, but something happened, and Micah moved away from Paradise Wells. He had returned later to take over his father's farm, but as far as Caleb knew, the man hadn't gone back to carpentry. Caleb wouldn't venture to ask the man to work with him. Micah King hated him.

Sixteen-year-old Jimmy Zook came to work for him over the summer. Caleb instructed the boy how to work with the wood and bring out its natural beauty. Jimmy was talented but had a way to go learning the trade. He used Jimmy to run errands and as an extra hand on demanding pieces. After another couple of years of apprenticeship, he would be a great person to have as an employee.

He and Jimmy loaded the wagon and headed the five miles to town. After unloading the toy boxes at the Thomas home, he offered to buy Jimmy supper at Lisette's, a small café on Main Street.

They entered the restaurant and found a table near the door. Lisette Duncan, the place's owner, hollered out to them across the room, asking what they wanted to drink. "*Kaffe* for me, Jah," Caleb said and nodded at Jimmy.

"A large Coke for me, please."

Lisette brought their drinks and took the supper order, then left the table. "I have a shipment of wood coming in next week, and I will need two wagons to haul it back to the shop." Caleb offered, then took a sip of his hot *kaffe*. It always tasted so good at this time of day. It gave him a pick me up to finish his work.

"Do you think I'm ready to make a rocking chair by myself?" Jimmy asked, hopefully. "I'm tired of making birdhouses and carving horses and buggies."

Caleb laughed, "So you feel you can do justice to a rocking chair? I have some oak in the back room. I might give you the chance to try out your skills with it."

Jimmy stood up as the nervous tension exploded from him. Realizing what he had done, he dropped back into the chair. "Sorry, boss, I'm just so excited that you are giving me this chance."

"You deserve it. You've worked hard the last few months, and you always listen to what I have to say. And you've come up with some good ideas yourself. Of course, I expect you to ask me for help if you get into a tight spot."

They had finished eating were nearly ready to leave when the doorbell rang as someone entered the café, notifying the servers they had new customers.

Caleb looked in the direction of the door, and there stood Eddie Vogel, looking down at Caleb. The older man had a grizzled look about him. He didn't wear a beard, and he wasn't clean-shaven either, more like he somehow sported a continual four-day growth of salt and pepper facial hair. His bushy gray eyebrows stood out over the top of his smudged glasses.

Eddie squinted at Caleb as he started to walk past the table where he and Jimmy sat. "Well, lookie here. Just the man I wanted to see."

Caleb held in a groan. The man liked to share tales. "Oh yeah? I'm sure you have some gossip you want to spread around?"

The older man kicked out his foot and dragged a chair over to where Caleb and Jimmy sat. "I sure do. It's something you'll want to hear." He sat in the chair he grabbed, leaned forward, and placed his chin on his folded hands. "You know that old girlfriend of yours, Iris King? Well, I dropped her off at her parent's house a bit ago. She doesn't look much different, but she wears English clothes now, so that should give you a hint about where she's been. I wonder what she's been up to all these years?"

Lisette came over to them with the *kaffe* pot in her hand. "Are you having something, Eddie? Or just visiting?"

"Nah, nothing for me yet. I'm meeting my wife here for supper. I suppose I better get us a table before the place fills up, and we have to wait."

Caleb was never so glad to see the man leave. His heart squeezed painfully in his chest. Iris. He loved her so much. He even asked her to be his wife, but she took off instead.

Caleb searched for Iris everywhere he could think of the night she went missing, but he never found her. He went home well after midnight and prayed she returned to her home as well.

The following day when he arrived at the King's, he found her mother crying and wringing her hands and her father stomping around the house, muttering about his daughter's Englisch ways.

Micah spun toward him. "You know this is all your fault! Iris sneaked in late, and she was a mess. I believe she even had a bruised cheek. Why did you do this to her when you found her? She must have fought you to stay away from her. After Sunday night and what I saw—the way—I *saw* you with my daughter!" Micah King scowled at him, and then he relaxed his face when his wife Naomi frowned at him. "Never come back here, is that understood?"

Caleb nodded at Micah and ran from the room and out the door. That was the last time he ventured near the King's home.

His heart broke. Why did Iris run away? Why did she have a bruised cheek? The questions circled his mind, and he couldn't make any sense as to what happened.

Nearly seven years passed, and he'd heard nothing from her or about her. Now, she was home. He didn't know how he felt about her return.

Jimmy sipped the last of his drink, making a slurping noise that pulled Caleb from the memories.

"I suppose we better be getting home, Jimmy." Caleb stood, tossed a few dollars on the table, and let the boy go first toward the door. All Caleb wanted to do was to drop Jimmy off and then head over to the King's. He wanted to know why Iris left him the way she did. He wasn't sure it was an intelligent thing to do, but no one hurt him as much, and he wanted answers from her. Now.

Caleb couldn't and wouldn't go to the King's to speak to Iris. Her father's words pealed through his mind. He supposed it didn't matter. Iris left him. She could come to him if she wanted. And he prayed she wanted to see him.

CHAPTER THREE

No one spoke a word after Iris's announcement.

Her father's face grew red in anger as he stared at her. Her brothers, Ben, and Jacob stood, then they rushed from the kitchen, leaving only her and her parents. Their silence grew long with just the sound of the wind-up clock in the nearby front room ticking away the seconds.

Finally, he spoke, "I need time to digest that you are back and that you have a child. Do you have a husband to go along with this child?"

She looked down at her lap, embarrassed, and shook her head. "No. Rose is mine, and mine alone. She has leukemia and needs your help. My only possibility is to set up a donor drive to find a match to donate bone marrow to save Rose, but family is better. Closer DNA."

The meeting with her parents was terrible. Worse than she'd expected. She said a quick prayer. *Dear Gott, please show my family mercy, not for me, but for Rose. She needs one of them to match. I don't want her to die, and you are the only one who knows the answers.*

Her *daed* grunted with disgust and remained silent for a couple of beats, then he said, "Go to your room. It is the same as you left it. I must think of all of this. We will discuss this in the morning after I've had time to pray about it." Then the hard lines of his face softened. "And Iris. I am glad to see you. This family has missed you much."

He stood, turned on his heels, and stomped from the room, leaving Iris and *maem* staring at each other.

"I would love to be with you and talk longer but do as your *daed* says. I will go to the barn and try to reason with *daed*."

Iris nodded and turned to leave the kitchen when *maem* said, "Do not forget we love you, daughter."

Iris never doubted her parents loved her. Her concern was they cared too much and that her leaving left a hole so deep in their hearts that it would be difficult for them to recover. "Thank you, *maem*. I love you all as well."

After retrieving her bag and purse from near the front door, she made her way up the stairs and found the door open to her room. One of her brothers must have done it to allow a bit of warmth from the stove in the front room to enter. As Iris stepped in, she gazed around the room, and tears filled her eyes. She'd been so happy here.

The bedroom was clean and tidy, and not a speck of dust lingered on her dresser or nightstand. The bedding looked tidy as well. Had her mother kept up the room on the off chance that she would return home at some point?

Iris dropped to the bed and let the emotions pour over her. The last time she was here, such turmoil filled her. The decision to leave the community hadn't come easy, but she knew she couldn't stay.

Sighing deeply, she opened up her bag and took out a picture of Rose. Her beautiful daughter wore a colorful scarf tied around her head to hide her bald head.

Micah paced around the barn. What a mess his family was in, and the knowledge that it was all his fault didn't help him feel any better. He knew Iris left for the city because of him. He shouldn't have told her she could never see Caleb again. Finding her and Caleb in the barn, he knew they were in love and would marry at the next marriage season. Earlier in the day, when he went to the mailbox, he'd found a letter from the State of Pennsylvania and opened it, not noticing it addressed to Iris. He saw she had taken a test to get her GED, something only the Englisch had use for, not the Amish. It wasn't their way. On top of it, he learned she was accepted to take college courses on the computer at the library once she completed her GED testing.

If she wanted to be Englisch as her actions spoke, why was she with Caleb? Indeed, he wouldn't agree to become Englisch.

All he could think of was talking to the Bishop. Bishop Eischler here in Paradise Wells was a fair man. He would listen and help guide him into a thought that made sense. Micah snatched his black felt hat from his head and smacked it against his leg with frustration.

He was heart sick when Iris spoke of her ill daughter. She said if they refused to help her, the hospital would put out a call for people to test their blood to make her little daughter Rose healthy again, but it might be too late to save her life. Then it struck him. Rose wasn't only Iris's daughter but his granddaughter as well.

This situation pulled at his pride. He growled into the quiet barn. Amish weren't prideful people, and it was a sin for him to feel this way. After all, he was a Deacon for the church. A minister to others, and now his soul needed a minister.

"Micah," Naomi whispered as she entered the barn through the walk-in door. "What are we going to do?"

Shaking his head, he didn't answer for a beat then said, "I'm going to talk to Ruben. He will guide me."

"We must tell her, Micah. We should have done this years ago."

He shook his head and gave Naomi a soft smile. "We did what we thought best for her, but now, *Gott* must want her to know the truth."

With that, he hitched his buggy and took off for the bishops.

The church leader's farm was on the outskirts to the north of the district and near his home. The turmoil running through his head caused dizziness that nearly toppled him from his horse. Shaking his head to clear it helped. His family had attended church gatherings in the district, which abutted this district, but when the northern section had a growth spurt, he and his family began with the Eischler group.

For over ten years, they worshiped in this district, and for eight of them, he was a Deacon.

As his mind swept the problems hammering it, he found himself turning up Ruben Eischler's road. Ahead was the barn, and the Bishop stood to welcome him. There was just the knowledge of someone to help give him support and talk to about Iris and now Rose. Ruben would offer him direction, relieve the tension and fear plaguing him ever since Iris had told them about Rose and her need for someone to help her.

"Welcome Micah, what brings you to my door at this late hour? I just saw to the animals." the Bishop asked. "Put your buggy by the barn and come inside for *kaffe*.

Micah did as the man instructed and followed his friend into the house. He shook off his coat and put it and his felt hat on a coat tree beside the door.

"I'll let Mary know we will be in the office and ask her to bring us some *kaffe*. I smelled some sort of baking earlier. I imagine she will share it with us." He smiled, and Micah saw the caring in his eyes. Yes, Ruben was his best friend and his Bishop.

Taking a seat on the overstuffed couch, Ruben sat across from him, his elbows on his knees and his fingertips tented. Looking over the top of them, he said, "You appear grieved, Micah. What is it?"

"Iris is back." Saying the words made his stomach flop. How would he ever tell his friend what he had learned earlier?

Micah heard the ticking of the wind-up clock as the silence multiplied in the room.

Finally, Ruben spoke. "There must be a grave problem to bring her back."

Micah nodded. "Yah. It is bad. You see, she has a daughter who is dying. She asked for our help. She wants our blood tested to find out if we can donate bone marrow to save little Rose's life."

Ruben's jaw dropped. "I see the problem you have. It is not because you want to deny her your help. It is because you cannot help."

He looked at the wooden floor beneath his feet and nodded. "I do not know what to do. That is why I'm here. I hoped you could give me some direction in this matter."

Mary walked into the room with a tray holding a *kaffe* pot and a plate of chocolate chip cookies. She set it on the table between the men, smiled, and turned around. When she left the room, she softly closed the door.

Ruben bowed his head while Micah watched Ruben's lips move softly through the prayer. Again, Micah listened to the clock tick away the seconds, the minutes, then when he thought his friend would never come out of his prayer, the clock chimed once to show the half-hour. The sound brought Ruben's chin up.

"*Gott* impressed on me that the truth shall roll out of everyone. The truth will set you free. All of you have many secrets. Remember to offer truth."

Micah took a deep breath. "I had a feeling you would tell me this. I hoped you would come up with a different way."

He shook his head. "There is no other way, my friend. Since this is an unusual situation, I can bring it up during our services on Sunday. There may be someone in the District who could help your granddaughter."

Micah felt himself go weak. He knew it was his pride, not an Amish principle, but to tell the whole district about his unmarried daughter and her daughter would be so embarrassing. To save Rose, he supposed it was a small price to pay. "*Jah*, well agree to it, if you think it a possibility to help."

Micah took a sip of *kaffe* and then reached for a cookie.

"It's all I can do. Hopefully, someone in our district will show up who will match. Did you say a drive for testing will spread through the state?"

Micah nodded. "That's what Iris said would happen if we didn't match Rose."

He and Ruben sat there enjoying the refreshment. Micah saw that it was full dark. He knew Naomi would worry if he didn't head home soon. "Ruben, I'd better go." He placed his mug on the tray, and he stood. The Bishop walked him to the door.

"My long-lost husband. I'm happy to see your return. I hope you have some answers for us." Naomi said as she stood from her chair at the table where she was darning socks.

Micah wrapped her in a hug. She was the most important person to him and had been for years ever since they'd met. Releasing her, he slid into his chair at the head of the table.

"Do you feel any better now?

He nodded.

"Yah, I do. he told me to forgive Iris as God already has. It is our one soul weakness. We must forgive her, and we must share the truth."

CHAPTER FOUR

The following day, Iris sat at the table. Her mother refilled the cup of *kaffe* for her and then took her plate to the sink, adding it to the other dishes awaiting washing. Iris wasn't a big eater anymore, but this morning, the biscuits, gravy, eggs, and orange juice hit the spot. She'd been so worried about her daughter, Rose, she hadn't taken the time for balanced meals. It showed in her hollow cheeks and her loose clothing. Iris swallowed down guilt. She should have removed the dishes herself and offered to fill her mother's cup. The tension in the kitchen was thick with anticipation.

Naomi slid onto the chair next to Iris. She sat quietly for a moment staring into her cup. Placing her hand over Iris', she asked, "Do you wish to tell me what's going on in your life? You said you want us to help save your daughter's life."

Iris turned her head and looked directly into *maem*'s eyes. "My daughter is in the hospital in Lancaster. She is dying."

"You told us last night that you have a dying daughter. Our granddaughter."

Iris nodded. "*Jah*, her name is Rose."

"*Ach*," Naomi cried. She threw her hands over her mouth, and tears flooded down her cheeks. "If I'd had more girls, I wanted to give them each a flower name, but...but I only had the boys after you."

"I remember. That's why I named my daughter for a beautiful flower."

Maem pulled a lovely, floral handkerchief from her dress pocket behind her apron. Flowers were her weakness. In the summer, the yard around the house had many flower beds, and not only did she grow vegetables to sell and to can, but she also had a flower garden. People came from miles around to buy her plant starts and flowers.

"Enough of my crying. Tears will not help anything. Tell me what's happening with your Rose," she said, sniffling and dabbed her eyes with the hankie.

Iris took a calming breath. Where did she begin? Iris never wanted anyone to know her reason for running away from home, hoping they would, instead, think she ran off with an Englisch boy. Iris couldn't lie to her *maem*, but she was determined not to give away any of her secrets. That was why only her family could help Rose. No one else.

"Rose has leukemia. That's a cancer of the blood."

"*Ach* no!"

"Not if I can help it." Iris's voice filled with determination. "The doctors said she needed a bone marrow transplant. I cannot give her mine."

Her mother shook her head. "I don't understand." Naomi gazed off in the distance focusing on the *kaffe* pot sitting on the wood stove.

Iris's fear and sadness from the past six years overtook her like a giant wave determined to pin her to the ocean floor. So much sorrow and pain she'd overcome to now face it again with her daughter.

"I am diabetic, and I cannot give mine to Rose. That's why I need to have my family take a blood test to see if someone is a match for Rose."

Maem's face paled as she listened. Then she drew Iris into an embrace, and their tears wet each other's shoulders. They sat there crying together when *daed* walked in from the mudroom. He'd kicked off his barn mud-covered boots and left his insulated coveralls hanging on a peg in the mudroom. How he'd washed up at the sink out there without them hearing him was a mystery.

He poured himself a cup of *kaffe* then dropped tiredly into his chair at the head of the table. "Are you ready to tell us why you left us and where you've been?"

Even though imparting the reason to *maem*, telling *daed* was another matter. "I'm here because my daughter needs a bone marrow transplant."

Maem quickly filled him in on Rose and Iris's situation.

Daed ran his work-worn hands through his blond hair. He looked as if he hadn't slept a wink last night. Lines marked the corners of his eyes, and she saw grey starting to blend with his light hair at his temples. He was forty-five, the same age as *maem*, and they were both breathtaking blonds. *Gott* blessed her and Rose with vibrant red hair and a lighter complexion than her parents. Her brothers had light brown hair and brown eyes. *Maem* had always said they were like mixed nuts. All different, but all wonderful.

"You will find no help here, Iris." His eyes narrowed, and his lips thinned, giving him a grim appearance.

"Daed! Please, I don't want Rose to die. You are my only hope to prevent it." A sob tore from her chest as she jumped from her chair. "Please..." her word trailed off and died in her throat. Strangely, his face drooped in sadness. She'd expected anger, but not this.

He snapped a glance at *maem*, and she nodded to him. "Daughter, please sit. I. We..." Again, he looked to his wife.

"Go on," *Maem* said, "She needs to know after all these years."

The way her parents were acting frightened her. "What do I need to know?" Iris's heart hammered in her chest and her tongue stuck to the roof of her mouth. She wanted to run out the door, but that would not do a thing for Rose.

Iris plunked back down onto the wooden chair.

"Iris. You. You are adopted."

The words zinged through her heart, and she bent forward and moaned as the air rushed from her lungs. "How can this be possible?" she asked, raising her head and darted her gaze back and forth between her parents.

Caleb tried to work on a kitchen cabinet, but his mind kept wandering to Iris. She left him years ago without a word or a note of explanation. Iris disappeared and left him with his heart smashed into shards. Why? He had told her how much he loved her, and she offered her sweet words of love in return. She'd even agreed to marry him. So, what caused her to flee? Was it the night they became intimate in the barn? She hadn't appeared frightened, only happy they were together.

However, the next day, she was gone.

These questions had circled in his mind every day six, nearly seven years. And now she was back. He slept little last night. All he remembered about Iris and why he loved her came back just as he started to fall asleep. He must have answers.

Tossing the screwdriver aside, Caleb walked away from his work and stepped outside. The morning was a bit cool, but the bright sun promised a warmer afternoon. He needed answers. He couldn't spend another day wondering why she left him.

Poking his head in the door, he hollered to Jimmy, "Would you stay here for a while if I leave? I have an appointment."

"One that is long overdue," he whispered under his breath.

Caleb fetched his horse and hitched her to his buggy. He would get answers from Iris, or he would not leave her family home. Daed wouldn't be happy with him. For some reason, his father didn't care much for Micah Fisher. All he cared about was questioning Iris. He had to know the reason she left him.

The Fisher farm was only two miles from the Miller's. It didn't take him long to reach their property. He guided the horse from the road to the long driveway beside the house. A thick grove of Maple trees lined the dirt road. It was interesting to see how their leaves were sparse now at the season's end, for only a couple of weeks ago, they had been thick and colorful. A few fell around him as a gentle breeze wished through the branches. The first snowfall couldn't be far away.

As he passed the corner of the house, he directed the horse toward the barn. People in their district used the back door where the mudrooms were handy to keep down dirt coming into the large front rooms. Before he could stop the horse, Micah King stepped out from the back of the house and stepped in front of him, taking the horse's harness in his hands, stopping her.

"You might as well turn around, Caleb. There is nothing here for you."

Caleb felt a sting in his face as he reddened. Nothing for him? Of course, there was. Iris likely was here. Where else would she go?

Caleb whipped his leg over the horse and jumped down, facing Micah King. "I'm here to talk to your daughter. Would you please tell her I'm here to see her?"

The older man stood with his hands on his hips, and his face pulled into an angry map of fine wrinkles. "*Nee*, I won't. You have no business with my daughter."

Micah kept his stance. For sure and certain, he wasn't letting him in to talk to Iris. "I don't know what your problem is, Mr. King, but your daughter is a grown woman. She can talk to anyone she desires to speak to."

Iris heard raised voices coming from behind the house. She walked through the kitchen and into the mudroom. What she saw froze her to the spot. Caleb. Why was he here?

Gossip must be popping up all over town, telling everyone that she was here. Now, what was she to do? Taking a calming breath, she opened the door and took the two steps leading to the ground.

As she did so, Caleb spotted her.

"Iris," he bellowed, "I want to talk to you."

The tone of his voice frightened her. Gone was the handsome boy, and in his place stood a powerful man, a very handsome one at that. Just seeing him standing there started her heart beating erratically, and her breath caught in her throat.

His gold-streaked auburn hair, always a bit longer than most of the Amish men, poked out from under his black hat. His golden-brown eyes surrounded by even darker brown lashes flashed at her. He had every right to hate her. She wished it weren't so, but it was. She loved him still. She always had. *Nee*, she couldn't hope to have him in her life again. It wasn't possible. She had her life, and he had his own life to lead, but she could dream about it.

"Please?" he called to her, more softly this time.

The tone of his voice pulled at her. She wanted to go to him, but finally, Iris shook her head and turned toward the door to go back inside. Even though it broke her heart to turn him away, she must. Too much had happened today. First learning of her adoption and now, Caleb?

Rushing back into the house, she intended to gather her bag and head back to the hospital and her daughter. She would tell the doctors to put Rose on the transplant list, and they would wait it out. She prayed her daughter would live long enough to have the procedure.

Maem stood from her place at the table. Iris could tell she'd been crying. It broke her heart to think of *maem* this upset. She realized now that she should have stayed here in Paradise Wells and not runoff, but at the time, Iris didn't have enough self-confidence to stand up for what she wanted. It wasn't the Amish way.

Iris sat down beside *maem* and took her hand.

"I'm so sorry for all this, Iris," *Maem* said, her eyes filled with tears, "if we could help you and Rose, we would. You still love Caleb, don't you?"

"*Jah*, I do. Now that I'm home, I see how much I miss it here. It breaks my heart to be away from you and the district, but I can do nothing about it. I have to work to cover the cost of Rose's medical care."

Her father stomped into the kitchen. "I wish you had never gotten involved with that man. He is no gutt, Iris. Stay away from him."

"I plan to do just that," she whispered. What concerned her more was, had *daed* heard what *maem* said? "Daed, do you know anything about my birth parents? If I can find them, maybe they could help Rose."

He shook his head. Her words calmed him a bit. Placing both hands on his wife's shoulders, he looked directly at Iris. "We don't know, daughter. We just don't know." He walked around the end of the table and sat across from them. This time, his eyes wore a glaze of sadness. "You deserve to hear the story of your arrival in our family, Iris."

Her heart pounded in her chest. She wanted to know, but then, she was afraid at the same time. "Yes, please tell me. Maybe it will shed some light on how I can help Rose."

He shook his head. "I wish it would help you both, but I fear there is no one to ask."

Naomi stood and walked across the kitchen, took three mugs from a cabinet, and grabbed the pot to fill them. First, she uncovered a plate of peanut butter cookies, then poured the cups full of *kaffe*. After two trips to the table, she sat. "This is a long story, and it will go down better with treats." She tried to smile at Iris, but the right side of her lips stayed down.

The differences at the sides of her mouth made Iris wonder if *maem* had been ill with a stroke.

"Yah," *daed* agreed. "It is a complicated story, indeed."

Iris remained quiet, and she knew he would tell her in his own time.

He leaned back in his chair and crossed his arms over his chest. "We didn't always live here, Iris. You see, I was born here, but I wanted to start a carpentry business, so I moved to a larger town where I could have more customers, near Steubenville, Ohio.

That's where I met your *maem*." He smiled over to his wife and affectionately touched her hand.

My *daed* was a farmer, but I did not enjoy the work. My heart was set on carpentry. My best friend was David Miller. Yes, you don't need to ask. Caleb's father. He was a few years older than me, but he worked with his father at the carpentry shop. I'd watch them work, and I wanted to learn, so his father took me on as an apprentice." He looked over at *maem* and smiled at her.

"Daed was not happy with my decision, but he didn't hold me back. Instead, he hired someone to help him at the farm."

I learned quickly and became quite good at woodworking. So much so that I wanted to start my shop. This area was smaller then, and there was no business for two stores, so I bid the Miller's and my family goodbye, and I moved to Steubenville.

"Tell her the rest of it, Micah," *Maem* whispered.

Daed's face reddened. "*Ach, Naomi!*"

Maem nodded, "Go on. She should know."

Daed placed his work-worn hands over hers. "I was courting Rebekah when David swooped in and took her from me. I couldn't stand to work with the man. I was determined to start up my shop in another place."

Rose felt her eyes grow wide at that bit of news. "Thank you for telling me this. It explains a lot."

Iris noted the play of emotions running across his face. After a few beats, his sadness changed to happiness. He took a sip of *kaffe* and broke a piece from the cookie, and popped it into his mouth before he continued. "Within a year, I was doing a good business, married your *maem*, and we were both happy with our life, but a tornado wrecked our lives in that little town." The memories he spoke of brought beads of sweat to his brow.

"Our house was on the outskirts of town. *Gott* saved us from the devastation brought on by that tornado. The storm flattened my business, though, and the community was a mess. We were sad but happy to have our home and each other.

A couple of days after the storm, the bishop came to us. The couple had a wee boppli with them, only two weeks old. Amazingly, the baby didn't die in the storm because her parents and grandparents died."

Iris leaned forward as *daed* spoke, taking in his words. "The boppli, was it me?"

"*Jah*, it sure was. You were a beautiful little thing. All big blue eyes and curly red hair."

"What about the family?" Iris asked.

The bishop told us the farm where the men worked was wrecked and all the records scattered to the wind. There was no way they could trace the family back to your people."

Maem added, "We fell in love with you, Iris. We have never thought of you as anything but our child. You are ours in every way." Tears again flooded her cheeks. "When you left us, it broke our hearts."

Daed nodded. "If you wish to come home with your daughter, we will welcome you. I'm sure the bishop and community will as well. You weren't baptized when you left. Others have rejoined their families here."

Iris shook her head. "I'm not sure it would work out. If we can pull Rose through this, she will need many doctor's appointments, and it's an hour's drive by car to Lancaster, all day by buggy on the back roads. Thank you, though." Their offer warmed her heart. She loved her parents so much.

Still, she harbored resentment toward her father. He had forbidden her and Caleb from courting. Why?

Iris had a return bus ticket, and she was to meet the bus in Paradise Wells at two o'clock. Her parents wouldn't hear of her calling the taxi to take her into town. Instead, her father insisted he take her in the buggy. Her mother went along, saying she wasn't going to let her daughter go like last time. She was returning to her daughter and job with their blessings.

On the bus back to Lancaster, Iris sat with her eyes closed and in prayer. Prayers for someone to come forward for testing and that someone to be a match. She also praised *Gott* for taking her home to see her parents. At least she had that much. She missed her family dreadfully. The only person missing was Caleb.

CHAPTER FIVE

Caleb drove his parents to David and Ruby Fisher's place for Church Sunday. It was a bit of a ride but traveling in the district every other Sunday was common. This day, snow threatened, and the weather had turned cold. Caleb bought a battery-operated heater to heat the buggy to keep everyone warm as travel was slow in the winter.

When they arrived, Ruby Fisher's son Matthew and her brother-in-law Levi tended to the conveyances, and everyone rushed into the house for the warmth.

The Fisher's front room had a divider wall that slid back, opening the dining area as well, so all the worshipers fit in the ample space. In two weeks, the Clovis home would host the services, and it was too small to use. The barn would have to do. At least farmers in the area had tall gas heaters to keep everyone warm. The problem they might meet was deep snow.

Caleb and his father walked to the benches' on the left, and his mother gathered with her women friends and girls on the right. The two sexes never mingled during the service,

For three hours, the Bishop and ministers took turns speaking. Finally, when he guessed everything was concluding for the day, Bishop Eischler spoke. "Everyone, before we end our meeting, I want to call Deacon King up to speak to us. He has an important message for us."

Caleb watched *maem*'s eyes widen with surprise, and her head snapped in *daed*'s direction. Messages during a meeting were not usual.

Visibly nervous, Micah walked to the front and began. "Friends, I humbly come to you with a request. Many of you know of my daughter Iris and that she left us a few years ago."

The congregation's voices filled the room with mumbling and whispers. Micah said nothing until everyone fell silent, and he started his plea again. "Iris has a daughter, Rose, who has leukemia. Her disease is bad. Our granddaughter is near the end of her life, and the only thing that can save her is a bone marrow transplant. None in our family are a match, and that is why we are calling upon you, our church family, to help us save her."

Bishop Eischler spoke up. "I want you to know I have permitted for any or all of you to take the test. Rose is in bad shape, and she needs this transfusion desperately. I have the forms for you to complete. All you have to do is take them to the hospital and have your blood drawn."

More murmuring followed.

"Ladies, gentlemen, please listen." The Bishop picked up a stack of papers and nodded to Micah. "Take the information as we hand it out. Someone in your family might match this little girl." Caleb took a form and passed it on. For sure and for certain, he would try to help Iris and Rose. He didn't move from the bench but sat ruminating when a thunderclap of realization struck him. Was this the reason why she wouldn't talk to him? She had a new family, and she didn't want to remember their old days together? Why didn't Iris' husband match his daughter?

His heart squeezed painfully, and he experienced a sensation that fell into his stomach. Caleb stiffened his spine to make himself shrug off the new information and not allow it to bother him. It wasn't working, however. Tears burned the back of his eyes. He'd never lost his love for Iris, and now hopelessness surrounded him.

The paper twisted in his hands. If he couldn't have Iris, he'd try to help that family with the testing. Someone somewhere had to match. At least he helped in some manner.

Following the meeting, well-wishers surrounded the King's, with over three-quarters of the people offering to help Rose. Caleb prayed they would show up for testing. If they couldn't help the little girl, they could match someone else and save their lives.

The next day all Caleb could do was think about Iris. Everything he did reminded him of her. They had gone to school together and had been friends ever since. It made no sense to him why she ran away.

Caleb thought he had put Iris in the past. He dated other Amish women, but he never felt close enough to them to get past a few buggy rides, then he called on them no more. He should have realized they didn't stack up to Iris.

He was angry at himself for not trying to go after her all those years ago.

"Caleb!" His father cried. "You are going to cut off your hand if you do not pay attention!"

He looked down to where he held the circular saw and found his left hand directly in the path of the screaming blade. Quickly, he released the trigger, and at once, the blade stopped.

Jumping away from the sawhorses, the tool and board fell to the ground.

"What a close call," David Miller said to his son. "What has been your problem recently?"

Caleb lost control of his anger and snapped, "It's none of your business, *daed*. Quit bugging me about it, will you?" Caleb was nearly as shocked as his father at this outburst.

"Fine. Do you want to cut off your hand? Be my guest, but I will not tolerate you screaming at me. Pay attention to your work or go to the house. Whatever you do, get over whatever demons have riddled your mind recently."

Caleb feared to say another word. His body trembled with fury. Tossing his gloves onto the sawhorse, he spun on his heel and stomped off. He went through the shop behind the house where he lived with his parents, then to the front where his horse and buggy were. In the buggy with one great step, he snatched the reins and flicked them to get the horse moving. He was going to Lancaster and get the blood test. Maybe his donation would help this deep sorrow.

After a good night's sleep and deep prayer, Caleb sheepishly entered the kitchen where his parents sat, sipping their morning *kaffe* and sharing a newspaper. He poured himself a cup and filled his breakfast plate with cheesy scrambled eggs, bacon, and a couple of biscuits. Having the testing out of the way made Caleb calm down. He knew that was all he could do for Iris and her daughter.

He neared the table, then sat across from his parents. "Daed, I'm so sorry about yesterday. I've been upset ever since Iris came back to her parents. Apparently, to get them to donate for her daughter."

His father looked over the paper and said, "You still love her, don't you, son?"

Caleb nodded. "It's in the past now, but when she showed up, it was like no time had gone by."

Maem patted his hand. "It's because you never had an ending. If you two had parted ways face-to-face, it would not be this way, son. As it stands, we realize everything hurts you."

"Well, thank you both for understanding. I will try not to take all this out on you. You don't deserve what I've been dishing out."

Daed gave him a long look and said, "And you don't deserve what she caused in your life as well. Now, what are we doing today?"

CHAPTER SIX

Caleb headed for town and his store. Daed was there, and he needed to talk to him about a call he received earlier on his cell phone. The Bishop allowed businesses to have technology as the outside world rapidly changed. They had to keep their businesses alive, and it was the only way they could compete.

A lot of recent sales at the storefront kept Caleb at a loss about what inventory was left. The woman calling today wanted a specific nightstand, and he wasn't sure if it was still in stock. He planned to work with *daed* and make a complete listing.

He and *daed* had a special relationship. Caleb not only loved him as a parent but as his best friend as well. There was no one else that gave him such comfort, except *Gott*, and even this relationship hadn't been as close as it once had been. Sure, he attended church, prayed, and enjoyed the people in his district, but something was missing.

When he entered the showroom, Caleb was surprised that he didn't see *daed* there, so he walked around the corner to the office area calling his name. He was on the floor beside the desk.

"Daed!" Caleb cried as he rushed to his side, kneeling. Checking the pulse in his neck, he found it to be thin and thready. *Nee*, this can't be happening. His mind felt frozen, and it took all his effort to stand. He pulled his cell phone from his pocket and dialed 911. Thankfully, the volunteer paramedics were close.

Staying by his father's side, each minute dragged on until he heard the ambulance siren. *daed* still had a pulse. Thank *Gott*!

The paramedics rushed into the showroom carrying bags and pushing a gurney. "Show us where he is." One man said matter-of-factually.

Caleb directed them into the office. Quickly they had *daed* on the gurney checking him out.

"How long has he been down?" A twenty-something girl asked.

He shook his head. "I found him this way when I arrived. He usually comes in around nine, so he could have been this way for up to two hours." Caleb's heart sank. Was his *daed* going to die?

The paramedics gave him oxygen, listened to his heart, then stuck leads on his chest hooked to a box with a jumping line showing on the screen. "It doesn't look like it's his heart, but we will send this EKG to Lancaster General."

Caleb nodded. "Ok, can I ride with you? I just have my horse and buggy."

Caleb?" Daed roused and tried to sit up.

Rushing to his father's side, he took his hand. "I'm right here. The ambulance people are taking you to the hospital."

"You can come along but in the front seat with the driver," the paramedic said. "We need the space in the back to care for your dad. We'll take good care of him."

"I have to tell *maem* what's happening." He ran his hand through his auburn hair.

The female paramedic said, "We will take care of it for you. I'll call dispatch and have a deputy go out to your house and tell her. They can even arrange a ride for her to the hospital."

"Thank you," Caleb uttered.

Shortly, the paramedics had *daed* loaded into the ambulance, and Caleb turned to the front of the ambulance as the girl took out a cell phone. This would be the longest ride of his life. Caleb opened the vehicle door and dropped into the seat, and placed the seat belt around himself. Never had he felt so alone.

Iris looked out the window of Dr. Rimmell's office after a lengthy discussion with him about her family background. Sadly, they both agreed it was imperative to put Rose on the donor list. Iris prayed someone would match her and soon. She loved Rose so much, and it tore at her heart that she could do nothing to make her well. This whole year had been a nightmare, ever since Rose's diagnosis. She knew it was all in the hands of God, but she wanted to sprinkle magic fairy dust over her daughter, cure her and walk out of the hospital.

Iris took the elevator down from the third floor where Dr. Rimmell's offices were. The door slid open into the Emergency Department where she worked.

The area sparkled with clean surfaces. The long hallway ran from the automatic entrance doors to the back elevator leading to the patient rooms. A floor up was glass cubicles. Curtains covered two cubicles, which showed a patient was within.

Iris let the charge nurse know she was in the building, and if they needed help, she would be available on the second floor checking on Rose. She had thirty minutes to spare before her shift started.

The elevator doors slid open. Iris stood at the back, and in front of her, the car was full of medical staff and visitors. She waited for the others to walk out and on to their busy days. She silently sent a prayer to them for a good day.

Rose's room was across from the nurses' desk. As she walked past, she waved at a nurse, Shelly Scott. They'd become friends while they were in nursing school. Walking up to the desk, she asked Shelly, "How was Rose's night?"

"She slept like a baby. Her fever stayed down all night. Of course, it will go up during the day when she becomes more active."

"Thanks for the update. I have just a few minutes before I have to start my shift, so I'd better get in there." She smiled and turned to face the glass wall behind her, which separated her daughter's room from the hallway.

She gowned-up and placed a mask over her face, then stepped into the room. Rose turned at the sound of the door opening. "Hi, mommy! I didn't think you would ever come. I miss you so much."

"Hi, snuggle bug." Iris leaned over and kissed her on the forehead through the mask. "You were asleep when I came to see you last night." She pulled up a chair and sat at the side of the bed.

The children's rooms had the beds closer to the floor, so it gave them the freedom to stand, and if they weren't attached to IVs, they could go to the bathroom on their own or play with the toys in the corner of the room. Rose, though, played on her iPad. She'd become weak and was getting IV fluids.

Rose looked her over, then smiled. "You have to work today, don't you? You're wearing your pajama clothes."

Iris nodded. Her baby always thought her scrubs looked like nightwear. "I'll spend my afternoon break with you today. I had to see your doctor, so they gave me an hour break this morning so I could do that."

Rose took her hand. "I'm glad you're back cuz I missed you lots and lots."

Iris reached over with her other hand and patted Rose's wrist. "I have no plans to be away from you, sweetheart. I missed you something awful as well. Would you like me to read to you before I have to go?"

Rose sighed. "I wish you could stay with me all day."

"Me too, and I will the next day I have off. Do you want me to order supper and eat with you this evening?"

"Oh, yes, mommy. That's perfect!"

"OK, I'll tell Shelly.

Iris smiled at her daughter's use of the word, perfect. It appeared to be the newest reiteration of the coined word awesome. Even at Rose's young age, she picked up everything.

Rose dosed off before Iris finished the short book. She smiled down at her daughter before she left the room. *Dear Gott, please find someone to help little Rose.*

After she told Shelly her plans for supper with Rose, she took the elevator to the first floor. She'd never used the elevator this much until Rose was a patient. Many of her coworkers gave her a sad smile, knowing the problems her daughter suffered. Iris imagined they all felt sorry for her and expected Rose to die at any time.

"Oh, Iris," The charge nurse called out to her, the woman's eyes never leaving the computer screen. HR wants you up at their office during your lunch break if you find time for one."

"Thanks," Iris called back. A sinking sensation captured her stomach. Every time Human Resources wanted her, it had something to do with her insurance. What could they be taking away now?

Sighing, she put the sad thoughts away, and in just moments, she logged into the hand-held computer and started her shift. The hand-held device tracked every movement and decision. Iris didn't mind as much as some of the others. It gave her confidence to make correct decisions. It was her backup.

"Incoming," someone hollered near the receiving bay. The sound of an ambulance backing toward the door announced its arrival.

CHAPTER SEVEN

Iris grabbed her stethoscope from the desk as she jumped up and rushed toward the paramedics as they wheeled someone through the glass ER doors.

Fifty-two-year-old male found down and unresponsive. Revived during the exam. Pulse 124 and thready."

"Take him into four. It's open," Iris said, directing the paramedics. "Dena," she sputtered to a nurse following her into the cubical, "call Dr. Clements and get him down here and let's get our patient's blood work, stat. I'll start the routine workup."

She glanced at the paramedic closest to her and said, "Shoot me over the EKG."

"Done."

Iris flicked her finger across the screen, and the results showed on her tablet. "Not remarkable."

She turned to her patient and looked up from her screen then and realized she knew this man. He was David Miller from Paradise Wells, Pennsylvania, Caleb's father.

"Mr. Miller, can you hear me?"

His eyes fluttered open. "*Jah*, I can hear you."

"Mr. Miller, I'm Iris King, a Nurse Practitioner here at General. We have called in Dr. Clements to see you. He is our heart specialist. He should be here momentarily."

He struggled to sit up. "Did I have a heart attack?" He asked, his voice shaking with tension.

Gently, Iris helped him lie back. "That's what we need the doctor to decide." She smiled at him. "Relax. That's the best thing you can do right now. Do you have any chest pains?"

"Daed!" Caleb rushed into the cubical, brushed around Iris, and went to his father's side. "The ambulance people told me *maem* is halfway here. It shouldn't take long the way Eddie drives in an emergency."

"For sure and for certain," Iris added under her breath.

Caleb turned to her. His eyes grew wide, and his brows raised with shock. "Iris? What are you doing here?" He looked her up and down and took in her Looney Tunes patterned scrubs and the stethoscope around her neck.

"I work here." She looked at her tablet as she spoke, trying to ignore that Caleb stood beside her.

She felt Caleb staring at her, which gave her goosebumps. After a moment, he spoke. "Are you a doctor?"

Iris laughed under her breath, "No, I'm a PA, nurse practitioner. Today, I'm overseeing the nursing staff on this shift."

A heavy-set woman with gray hair walked up behind Iris and said, "Is that right? What am I doing then?"

"Following my orders," Iris said lightly. "Mr. Miller, this is our charge nurse, Mrs. Taylor. She'll be helping us run any tests the doctor wants."

At that moment, a short, thin man with wire-rimmed glasses and a receding hairline came around the curtain. He held his tablet in his hands. "You gave everyone quite a scare, Mr. Miller."

The charge nurse told the Miller men, "This is our cardiologist, Dr. Clements."

Caleb nodded in recognition. "Did he have a heart attack?" Caleb asked.

"The blood work will be the definitive proof we need. The EKG done on the way here doesn't show anything peculiar. There are a few gaps here and there, though."

The Dr. approached his patient and placed a hand on David's shoulder. "I have a few questions for you, Mr. Miller." He pulled up a tall stool and looked down at his tablet. "I see you are 52 and that you are Amish. Do you have any medical problems I should know about?"

David shook his head. "*Nee*."

Iris caught the warning look he shot his son.

"Daed, this is not a time for secrets. If you don't want the district to know, that's fine, but don't evade the man's questions. He's here to help you."

"Alright." The word had an angry tinge to it. "I have Parkinson's disease," he said and closed his eyes as if admitting his physical problem would cause the sky to fall in on him.

The Dr. tapped his tablet. "Well, that explains a whole lot. "Mr. Miller, tell me. Had you been sitting then standing rapidly when all this happened?"

David frowned as he thought about the question presented to him. "I took a few steps after I stood, then I don't remember anything until my son stood over me."

The doctor nodded. "With Parkinson's, it can give you exceptionally low blood pressure. Let's see what your labs have to say before I offer you a diagnosis." He looked at Caleb. "You can stay with him, and I'll be back as soon as I know more."

Caleb snapped his gaze at Iris. She nodded. "I'll direct your *maem* here when she arrives." She walked out with the doctor, leaving David and Caleb alone.

She hadn't reached the nurses' station when another ambulance arrived. Rushing around, she looked at her tablet and found an open cubicle.

The paramedics burst through the door. "Nine-year-old boy. Drowning victim. CPR started at the scene."

Iris began to direct both nurses and the paramedics down the hall to the available cubicle.

After thirty minutes, Iris came out from the boy's room and slowly walked toward the nurses' desk. The boy hadn't made it. Children got to her the worst of all deaths. She hadn't made it there when Rebekah Miller ran up to her and asked for information about her husband.

"Mrs. Miller, he's just across the hall. Let me take you to him." Touching the older woman's elbow, Iris walked her to the cubical covered by the curtains, pulled shut for privacy. She opened the door, stepped around the curtains, and said, "Look who I found in the hall."

"Rebekah!" David shouted as Caleb interjected, "*Maem*!" at the same time.

"How is he?" she questioned at no one in particular, her eyes wild with a frantic look.

"He is good," Caleb said. "The doctor will know as soon as his labs come up on his gizmo. Something that everyone around here carries."

"It's each of our patients' charts. All the lab work, x-rays, any number of tests are sent to us. We can find out whatever problems our patients have in just a few minutes." Iris offered.

Caleb stood to let his parents sit together. "It sounds like magic to me."

Iris left the cubical and returned to the nurses' desk. Now she was away from the Miller's, her heart began thumping loudly in her chest, and her hands shook.

"Are you OK?" Bob Carter, a second-year resident, asked her.

She nodded. "I'm still upset we couldn't save that drowning victim. Nine is too young to die."

Bob sat beside her, reached under the countertop, and opened a small refrigerator. He handed her an ice-cold water bottle. "Maybe you should take a break."

"No. I came in an hour late today. I had to meet with Rose's oncologist before my shift. I'll eat with her later."

He shrugged and stood when another ambulance backed to the receiving doors. "You stay put. I'll cover this one. You take the next."

"Thanks. I need it."

Bob rushed off to the paramedics, asking the questions he needed to begin his assessment.

Iris' iPad dinged, which usually meant a report came into one of her patients' charts. Swiping across the screen, she saw David Miller's labs had arrived, so the doctor should be here shortly. Right on cue, he rounded the hallway leading to ER.

"You ready to go see David Miller with me?"

Iris stood and followed him into the cubicle.

"Good news! Your blood pressure bottomed out, causing you to faint, then you hit your head against the floor. Miss King checked you for a concussion when you arrived, and you have no signs of that either."

David sighed and winked at his wife. "Go call a taxi. I want to go home."

"Not so fast," the doctor interjected. "I want you to stay overnight. We need to do a few tests before I release you. You'll need medication to control this blood pressure issue, and I need more information before I prescribe meds."

David nodded with understanding. "Caleb. Get *maem* home." He then looked at the doctor and asked. "Can you tell me what time tomorrow you'll let me go?"

The doctor raised his brows, looked at his watch then spoke. "Let's say you have a ride here at five tomorrow evening. I'll have the reports back by then, and I'll meet with you and get you set up with meds and an appointment schedule."

Rebekah spoke quietly. "So, he will be OK?"

"Yes, Mrs. Miller. It was quite fortunate he had this issue while he wasn't doing anything dangerous." He stood and said, "I'll leave you in Iris's good hands. She'll arrange for your room and the tests. You both," He looked at Rebekah and Caleb, "might as well go. There isn't anything you can do right now. We'll be busy for the next hour or so."

The doctor walked out, and Caleb hugged his father. "I'll be right outside the room. Take your time with *daed*," he told *maem*.

"I'll go arrange for your room, Mr. Miller." She followed Caleb out the door.

As she exited, Caleb grabbed her elbow. "Please, Iris, I need to talk to you."

Iris tried and failed to leave the room quicker than Caleb, but her attempt failed miserably. She didn't want to talk to him. Not here. Not now. Her heart raced in her chest. Being this close to Caleb pointed out that she wasn't over him. Not even a little bit. They had always been close. From the time they were kinner and their mother's visited each other.

They had played on the swing set in the side yard, and when they were older, helped each other's parents, whether in the barn with the animals or in the kitchen peeling potatoes. They were always together.

For the past six years, Iris kept busy working and gaining her education and finally, getting the hospital job. She cared for others, and it broke her heart to see the pain in Caleb's eyes. The realization that she had hurt him badly gave her pangs of guilt.

She could not have stayed with her parents. Her father's anger and distrust were as good as a shunning. Her only choice had been to leave.

Now, she had no idea who Rose's father was. She prayed it was Caleb, but God hadn't given her the answer she needed. If she knew for sure, she would consider returning to the Amish. She missed the Amish ways so much. The Englisch life was difficult.

Iris took a breath, ready to break his heart with sharp words that were sure to keep him away when the emergency room door flew open, and paramedics rushed a woman on a gurney toward her.

"Female, age 66, cardiac arrest we restarted her on the ambulance."

Iris bounded down the hallway to the first open cubicle leaving Caleb standing open-mouthed as he watched her. Iris felt his gaze upon her back.

Thirty minutes later, the medical team had the woman stabilized when Iris left her patient to the cardiologist. Glancing around, she'd found Caleb and his parents were no longer in ER. Hopefully, Caleb wouldn't return to ER and find her.

The ER quieted in the early afternoon, and Iris clocked in her lunch hour. They used the time-clock system for lunch breaks not because the staff abused the time but for documentation that the break was cut short. The extra hours added to their paychecks.

Iris took the elevator to the third floor. Most of the offices were on that floor. HR was a small office having no space for chairs. Someone placed a string of chairs outside the office door for a waiting area and gave privacy to people in the main office.

Today she was the only person. The tiny outer room had a table with a phone on it. Nothing else. Iris wondered if this whole office had been a storage closet as she picked up the receiver and the phone rang in the office manager's office. "Iris, come on in," the woman said.

She saw her behind the glass door waving at her. Taking a calming breath, Iris walked toward the door, then quickly opened it. She didn't want to hear about insurance today, but she must know. Whatever it was, Iris expected it to break into her ever-decreasing check.

"Take a seat."

Iris saw this wasn't the usual older woman. This girl looked younger than she was. The nameplate on the desk showed "Sam Watters." Even her name sounded young.

"The reason I needed to see you today is for your contract renewal. You are within the three-month end period, and the board reviewed your work. In these downward economic times, they have chosen not to renew your contract."

Iris sat there silently, imagining cricket sounds. She had no response to this news. If she didn't have a job, Rose would have no insurance at all and no way to pay Rose's medical bills?

"Iris. I know this is a shock to you."

"You think?"

"The other thing, a better bit of news is this. The board wants to keep you on. A few openings are coming up in different departments. When something comes up, they'll offer you a job in another area of the hospital."

This roller coaster ride came to an abrupt stop. "I could get out of ER?"

Sam laughed lightly. "Yes, but you might have to wait for an opening. There is no guarantee a job will open at the end of your contract. I hope this won't be a hardship to you. Of course, the board knows about your daughter's illness, and your insurance will stay in place."

Relief flooded Iris. As long as the insurance was in effect, she could take her skills to a medical office short term. It would be a way for her and Rose to survive.

"Thank you for all the information, Ms. Watters. How will I know when there is a job offer?"

"I have all your contact information on the computer. I'll just give you a call and follow it up with another contract which will outline your work hours, wages, etc."

Iris stood. "That'll work, and now, I'd better get moving if I plan to eat something before going back on the floor. Thank you for this."

The girl nodded and flashed her a big smile.

Once Iris was out of HR and headed for the cafeteria on the ground floor behind the ER department, her heart returned its regular rhythm. What a scare. The thought of no job terrified her, but right now, all she could do was work out her contract and pray another job would come in for her.

Caleb helped his father from the taxi car and up the three steps into the mudroom, with *maem* following close behind. "Help him into our room, son. I will be right there to help him to bed."

David stopped in the middle of the kitchen. "I will not be helped to bed like a boppli. I am home now, and I want some *kaffe* and a nice piece of pie before I take to my bed. Spending the night and all today in the hospital leaves a man starving. Their tiny pieces of food and *kaffe* so weak you can barely tell what you are drinking."

"Daed..."

"No, son, let go of me."

When Caleb released *daed*'s arm, the older man stepped to the head of the table and pulled out his chair. "This has been my place for over thirty years, and I plan to live here for thirty more."

"Ok, have it your way. Will you be okay *maem* if I go into the store to check on my orders?"

She nodded as she turned the burner up under the morning's *kaffe*. "For sure and certain. I can handle *daed*, and I'll help after the evening snack.

"I'll be back within the hour."

"Good, I'll have supper on the table."

Caleb shook his head. "You two eat what you want. Surely, there are leftovers in the refrigerator. I'll grab something when I get home. We've had a long couple of days."

Maem set a plate of peach pie in front of *daed*. "If you have a piece of that left, I'll have it with a big glass of milk when I get home." He turned and walked out the back door.

He hitched the family horse to the wagon and started for town. The sun set, and only a bit of faint pink colored the late fall sky. The color brought Iris to his mind, and her cheeks were so rosy, like the sky. Why wouldn't she talk to him? What he wanted to know was why she left a few years back. Why did she try so hard to avoid him?

CHAPTER EIGHT

Iris awoke with a sound interrupting her dream. Grasping at the thin wisps of sound, it dissolved into the mist as she came awake. It was her day off. Why was someone calling her at—seven o'clock? She'd been so busy the past two weeks since she returned from Paradise Wells. Her dream continued to fade. All she remembered was Caleb's face.

"Hello...?" The sleep-filled word groaned from her throat. Water, she needed water. Opening one eye, she spotted last night's water bottle on the nightstand near her phone. She sat up in bed and reached for it.

"Iris?"

The man on the other end sounded uncertain if he had reached the right person.

"This is Iris."

"Oh, it didn't sound like you. I woke you up, didn't I."

She nodded, then realized he couldn't see her reply. "Yes. It's my day off."

"Good. Oh, this is doctor Rimmell. I am calling to tell you that we may have found a donor for Rose."

His words brought her fully awake now. Tossing her hair out of her face with one hand while holding the phone cleared her vision. She took a quick drink of water.

"A donor? Oh my gosh. When can we schedule her procedure? What's next?"

"You'll have to sign the papers for us to proceed. We'll contact the donor and get him in here to sign as well."

There was silence from Iris. Was this a dream? Could it be possible?

The doctor took over when Iris didn't respond. "Iris? Are you still there" Iris felt a lightness flow from her toes to the top of her head. Her heart fluttered. Delight filled her. Pictures zinged through her mind. Iris envisioned a happy life for her and Rose as Amish. She could see it all now.

Just as quickly as the pictures rushed at her, they dissolved into a dark area of her mind. She couldn't go back there. There were too many obstacles to a plan like that. No, she had the fantastic job she loved and her daughter.

"Iris, are you there? I know this has been a shock to you and pulling you from your sleep on top of it, but could you get down here soon? We need to begin this. Rose had an awful night."

She jumped out of bed and ran to her closet, and rummaged through the clothing. "Thanks, doctor. I'll be there as soon as I can."

"Good. I'll tell Stacey to let you right into my office when you get here." The phone went dead.

Iris held her clothing to her chest, and she spun in circles around the room.

She had so many questions, but she felt helpless to find answers for them.

CHAPTER NINE

Caleb entered the shop when he heard his phone ringing. When he was working, he left it on the desk because woodworking was a dirty business. It had to be early yet, not much after seven o'clock. His heart raced with fear. He's only had bad news with calls like this.

Swallowing hard, he took long strides to reach the phone before it could stop ringing. He haltingly reached for the telephone. Unsure if he wanted to answer it. He punched the answer button. "This is Miller's Fine Furniture, Caleb speaking."

"Caleb, great! You're the man I needed to speak with. This is Dr. Joseph Rimmell at Lancaster General Hospital. I have good news for you, son. You are a match for Rose King!"

The doctor's words took the starch from his legs, and he dropped into his desk chair. It was a good thing it had a padded seat.

He took a deep cleansing breath. His mind spun with the news, and disbelief filled him. "I am? Uh, ok." His mind whipped in a frenzy as he tried to focus on what the doctor said. Was he a donor? "What do I do now?" he asked breathlessly.

"We need you to sign the required paperwork. I also want you to know the risks involved in what you are doing."

"Risks? Are there side effects for Rose and me as well?" he asked the doctor. Of course, he would do anything for Rose and Iris. He was worried about the little girl. That is why he got tested.

"I'll go over all of this when you arrive. I'll let the receptionist know to expect you."

Iris arrived at the hospital in less than thirty minutes. Her heartbeat slammed against her ribs, and she didn't know to be excited or afraid. The feelings were all rolled up in one. Prayers to God filled her mind. Please keep my Rosebud safe and give her glowing health back.

Finally, the doors opened, and she stepped aside for all the people to come out. Business workers and medical staff blended into a whirling stream. When they finally exited, she entered the box filled with the smell of medicine and various perfumes and aftershaves.

Her stomach flipped. She couldn't become sick with nerves. Reaching into her carry-all bag, she drew out a water bottle, uncapped it, and took a healthy drink. It filled her empty stomach, and nausea abated.

Six people entered the elevator, and one pushed the button she needed. Standing at the back of the car, Iris leaned against the cold steel and closed her eyes. A picture of Rose healed and playing in their playground across from their apartment filled her thoughts. She had to stay positive, not wanting to draw any negative energy to her and her daughter. There were enough problems without concocting more of them from fear.

The elevator stopped and started, and people left the car. Finally, only she and another woman remained.

As the door opened, they both stepped out. Iris going straight ahead, and the woman to the right, headed to the only office in that direction. Financial aid. Iris visited there many times throughout Rose's illness. Her insurance covered eighty percent of the medical costs, but that last twenty percent built to a skyrocketing number. She had no idea how much this bone marrow replacement would cost. Of course, Rose's life meant more to her than any amount of money.

Iris took a deep breath and opened the glass door etched with the words, Dr. Carlton Rimmell. She saw him sitting at his desk.

"Hi, Iris," the receptionist said. "The doctor said to have you come right in when you got here. I hope you hear good news today." The girl had been at the reception desk all the times Iris brought Rose for her appointments.

"Thank you, Stacey. I hope it's going to be the best news ever."

Iris stepped in the direction of the doctor's office with shaking knees and a dry mouth. She had to find out about the donor's test and how close of a match they were. Hopefully, the match was seventy-five percent or more. That was the breakpoint, so she knew they had to be that close. The higher the number, the better the outcome would be for Rose.

She tapped lightly on the door, and Dr. Rimmell called out for her to enter. Opening the door, she saw out across the city of Lancaster. The morning sun glinted off the glass.

"Come on in and take a seat," the doctor said as he stood to face her. He had a broad smile on his face and a row of even, white teeth gleaming from it.

"It's true? Rose will get her bone marrow transplant?" Iris dropped onto a leather chair with arms and a high back. The softness of the leather cuddled around her, making her feel supported and more relaxed. She laughed inwardly, supposing this was the whole idea of the supple material. She wondered how many other people sat here and had faced the bad news of their children's impending illnesses.

"Yes, we did get lucky this time. I'll give you more information in a minute. Let me finish my notes here, and I'll be right with you to give you my undivided attention. It should only be a few minutes. Would you like coffee while you wait?" The doctor motioned to a cabinet across the room with a pod coffee maker and a wide choice of coffees.

She nodded. "It certainly will give me something to work on while you finish your work."

The hot water gushed into the black mug and made steamy sounds as she stood there watching. When the final drip splashed into the coffee mug, she moved it to a spot on the counter, opened a creamer pod, and added it to soften the sharp taste.

She was stirring with a wooden spoon and watched as the coffee became a caramel color. She took a sip so the coffee wouldn't spill as she turned to walk back to the chair.

Someone rapped on the door and at once stepped into the room. Doctor Rimmell looked up from his work. "Yes," he asked.

"I'm Caleb Miller. You said you wanted to talk to me about being a donor for Rose King?" Doctor Rimmell's eyes grew wide, and he pushed himself up from his chair. "How did you get in here. Didn't Stacey tell you I was busy at the moment and to have you wait?"

The secretary rushed past Caleb and gushed apologies to the doctor. "I'm so sorry! I was in the copy room and didn't see him arrive."

The doctor closed his eyes and shook his head. "It is against our policies to have the donor and the recipient families meet."

Stacey took Caleb's arm, but she couldn't budge the man. Then turning, he saw Iris only a few feet away.

"Stop," Iris said. "It's too late to unsee him. Just let him into the room."

Iris wished he weren't so handsome in his dark slacks, black vest, and blue shirt. Strong and beautiful. He was manly now —much more than when she'd had left.

Dr. Rimmell reached over his desk and put out his hand for a shake. "Please have a seat. We have many things to discuss."

Caleb turned toward her, and she saw a wave of anger in his eyes she had never seen before. Realizing she was the reason for this reaction wasn't easy to face.

Caleb said nothing, and he turned his attention to the doctor.

"Sit, Mr. Miller. Iris, come on over and join us."

Tentatively, she took small steps and neared the leather chair. Now was the time to face so much she'd swept under the rug. At least she knew Caleb was Rose's father.

Opening a file, the Dr. began. "I'm not sure how much you know about Rose's illness, Mr. Miller."

"First, can you tell me if Rose is my daughter?" Caleb asked Dr. Rimmell. His voice growled out low and sharp.

Dr. Rimmell's eyes grew wide, and his lips pinched into a wrinkle. His eyes darted between Iris and Caleb.

Caleb shook his head and looked down at the floor. "Or better yet, why didn't you tell me, Iris. I would love to know the answer."

Silence filled the room.

"Shall we begin this again, Caleb...Iris?"

Iris took a deep breath and said, "Yes. Caleb and I can talk after this meeting. Is that OK with you, Caleb?"

He nodded, but his face etched with lines of displeasure.

"Alright then," Dr. Rimmell took glasses from the top of the desk and placed them on his nose, and looked through a stack of papers in the folder. "Mr. Miller, you are a 98 percent match with Rose. That's the closest number we've had in years."

A gust of air burst from Iris, and relief flooded her body. "So Rose is going to live, barring anything unforeseen. Is that what you're saying, doctor?"

"I'd say she has a greater chance of survival now. There are no guarantees, but before you came forward, Mr. Miller, she had no possibility at all."

"How long will this take?" Iris asked. She hoped it was soon because she worried that Rose didn't have much more time left. She had been given chemo nearly two weeks ago in preparation for a stem cell transplant, with the doctor hoping a match would come about from their donor drive.

The Dr. leaned back in his chair, tented his fingers in front of him, and looked at Caleb. "Mr. Miller, we can do this in a couple of days if you are ready and have a plan for the next two weeks as you recover."

Caleb looked from the doctor and to Iris. "Can you tell me about the process? I volunteered my blood, but I don't know how it all works."

Doctor Rimmell, with his elbows on the desk, leaned forward to address Caleb. "You're positive then?"

"*Jah*, I will do whatever is necessary to make sure Rose gets better. Just tell me what to do and when to be here."

Caleb sat facing the doctor. He hoped he could understand what the man told him, but all he could hear was a buzzing in his ears with words faintly running through them. Shaking his head to help clear his mind, Caleb said, "Doctor Rimmell, sir, can you give me a moment? All of this has been a shock to me." he swiped his hand through his hair, allowing the cool air in the room play against his scalp. Sweat beaded his forehead, and he wiped it away with his hand.

"I know this is difficult, Caleb," Iris whispered to him.

He snapped his head toward her, and his spine stiffened in anger. "*Nee*, you can have no idea how I feel. You have robbed me of years with my daughter, and now she may die without me getting to know her."

The doctor spoke up. "You are here, Mr. Miller, to save your daughter's life. I suspect you will have many years to know her, and I can assure you she is a delight, much like her mother."

He didn't want to hear glowing words about Iris. He had loved her once, but at this moment, he didn't feel anything beyond a storm of disgust. How could she have done this to him as well as to Rose?

"I think I have my mind cleared now. What do I need to do?"

"Nothing more than a complete physical to make sure you are healthy enough to donate. Here is a card for our clinic across the street." He pushed a button on the phone and spoke after a female voice said, "Yes, doctor?"

"Would you contact medical oncology? I'm sending Mr. Miller over there in a few minutes for a donor physical."

Caleb breathed out with a sigh. He'd never had a physical and was unsure of what took place. The Amish went to doctors, but only if they had a problem, which he never had during his twenty-six years.

He nodded, then asked, "Is that all there is to it?"

"That's it. Of course, on the day of the transplant, there will be much more. You will be in an outpatient surgery room. We will give you general anesthesia and use a needle into both sides of your hip bones to withdraw the bone marrow. We will use this to infuse Rose. So that you know, your daughter has undergone chemotherapy to wipe out her defective cells completely so yours can replace hers.

"It sounds like a miracle."

"It is. I know the Amish are strong believers in faith and God. I am not Amish, but I am a believer as well. I've always felt God sent this procedure to heal the children."

Caleb's worries eased after hearing the doctor speak.

"Go on and head over to the clinic. They will be waiting for you."

The men shook hands, and Iris said, "Would you like me to show you the way?"

"*Nee*, I would rather find it myself. I don't need you for anything, Iris."

"Is there a way my office can contact you when we are ready for the procedure?" Dr. Rimmell asked Caleb.

"Jah, I have a cell home for my business."

"Alright. Just give the information to Stacey as you leave, and we will set it all up and let you know the specifics. It all depends on what we find out during your physical. Your tests should be in tomorrow."

"Is it alright to tell Rose?"

The doctor paused as he thought about the situation then offered, "I see no problem with it. This young man appears in good health, and I expect no problems that would keep him from donating."

Caleb held the door open for Iris and followed her out. When he stopped at the reception desk, she continued going out the door and into the hall. For as angry as Caleb felt, seeing her leave pulled at his heart. *Nee*, he told himself. You don't need her kind of love. She is my daughter's mother. Nothing more. He wondered how many times he would have to tell himself this before his heart responded to the feelings.

CHAPTER TEN

Iris watched Caleb from a window in the third-floor hallway as he navigated the crosswalk heading for his appointment. She didn't know what to do. The whole situation rattled her emotions. Happiness filled her to know that Caleb was Rose's father, one of her attackers. With this knowledge, she could put the terror behind her. Iris poked at the memories with an imaginary pin and willed them away and prayed they would never return. The memories of her father's barn and she and Caleb meeting there each Saturday night made her smile. Rose was conceived in love. Knowing this gave her a sense of happiness not tainted with sad recollections.

She heard the distant sound of a phone ringing, bringing her back to reality. She wanted to visit Rose. It was early still. Hopefully, she had enough time to order a breakfast tray to have delivered to her daughter's room. They hadn't shared breakfast in a long time. Additionally, she planned to tell Rose of the impending transplant.

Her daughter was a bright girl and knew every step of the way the diagnosis led. She also knew what a bone marrow transplant meant for her recovery.

Iris walked back into the doctor's outer office. "Stacey, would you call down to the dietary department and order a tray for me so I can have breakfast with Rose?"

Stacey smiled over at her, then picked up her receiver, punched a button, and started talking.

In a few moments, Iris stood in front of Rose. She watched her beautiful daughter sleep. Her long red eyelashes and fine brows were gone, along with her curly, red hair, which mimicked her own. Rose was self-conscious and wore a warm, fine knit hat. She could wear a wig as so many other young girls did, but not Rose. She was independent and didn't like the way the wigs felt and looked. After trying on a short curly wig, she whispered to Iris that she looked like the grandmotherly volunteer, Mable, who read stories to the children. She and her daughter laughed and laughed. That was the end of the wig idea.

Next came the silky scarves. They were a bust as well. The material wouldn't stay on Rose's head. All she did was fuss with them and finally balled them up and tossed them into a drawer in her cabinet wall.

Finally, a young woman came through with the knitted beanies. Rose loved a light pink beanie. Iris bought her two. One to wear and one for the wash. Now the girl covered her head without aggravation.

"Mommy! Guder mariye!"

Iris smiled. She taught Rose a few words in both Pennsylvania Dutch from the time she could walk. Deep in her soul, Iris wanted her daughter to know her grandparents and uncles. The problem was to get Rose into the Amish world. Would the district reject her and thus shunning Rose as well?

"Guder mariye to you, my beauty."

Rose giggled then became serious. "Mommy, I was so sick last night. I saw an angel. He said he would come for me when it was my time to meet Jesus. I'm scared." The little girl reached out her arms for a reassuring hug from her mother.

Iris grew up and reached for her daughter. Her heart squeezed painfully. She prayed the transplant would come fast before that angel had a chance to show up and take her baby away.

Freeing herself from Rose's hug, Iris sat on the edge of the bed. "I have some good news for you. The doctors have found a donor for you. The transplant could happen in a few days."

Rose's eyes widened. "Really? Does that still mean I will get better and get to go home?"

Iris nodded. "You will still need to be in the hospital until the procedure works and you start making new blood cells. But we hope that won't take long."

"That's the bestest news I've ever heard."

The door opened quietly, and one of the dietary managers walked into the room. "Looks like it's mommy-daughter day. I brought you both our full breakfast. Someone let the news out they found a donor for this wonderful girl, and we all know that Rose will get better fast."

Rose tossed her legs from under the covers then pulled the bed tray across her lap. "Come on, mom, get ready."

Iris followed her daughter's example, and soon they devoured eggs, bacon, and toast along with a big glass of orange juice.

Caleb watched mother and daughter from the safety of the nurses' station. He was glad both Iris and Rose were laughing and having a good time, but he felt like an outsider. Somehow, he would find a way to become Rose's friend, even if he couldn't be part of her life.

A week passed before doctor Rimmell told Iris the bone marrow transplant was the next day at eight a.m.

Everyone in the hospital knew of the struggle with Rose's health. With the transplant upon them, her supervising doctor, Brian McCloud, wasn't surprised to see her. "You must have a date for Rose's transplant," he said off the cuff and looked up from the paperwork on his desk and into her eyes.

Iris nodded. "Yes, it's tomorrow. I'm here to ask for a week off to be with Rose."

"I'm more concerned about your health at the moment, Iris than I am Rose's recovery. You're worn out. Is there somewhere you can go close to here where you can relax the rest of the day? I don't want you in ER. Wind down, so you're strong for Rose."

"You want me to take today off as well?" she hadn't expected this. "My apartment is nearby. I walk to work every day. It's only a five-minute trip."

"That will work, but when Rose is released, I hope you two can catch a plane somewhere and spend a couple of great weeks together recovering from this nightmare."

Being with her daughter would be enough. She pondered if the apartment would bother Rose. Her daughter spent weeks there horribly ill before she had to go to the hospital. Iris knew the oppression which tried to strangle her each time she opened the door. Would Rose feel this as well?

"I'll get someone down there to cover for you. Are you sure a week is enough?"

"What? Are you trying to get rid of me, Doctor?"

The man laughed and walked around his desk and approached her. He was short, round, and probably in his early sixties. Grandfatherly.

"Finish your shift and go to Rose. Even though she is excited, you know she must be terrified as well. I sure would be." He smiled at her. "This is her second chance. She'll make it."

Rose nodded. "I pray to *Gott* that is his desire. I'm scared as well, and I'm her *maem*."

"*Maem*?"

"Oh, sorry, the Amish vernacular is coming out. Any time I'm around Amish patients, I revert to my old ways."

"Go then. Be with your daughter. I will track both of you. If you need me for anything, ring me up, and I'll be there for you both."

Iris planted a quick kiss on his lined cheek and then walked from the room.

CHAPTER ELEVEN

The medical staff took Rose through the door leading to the procedure suite. Iris tried not to cry and upset her daughter, but with her out of sight, the tears flowed. She watched, rooted to the floor, until the nurses turned the corner, and she could no longer see her baby. Telling herself the procedure would bring health to Rose calmed her a bit, but she knew that things occasionally went wrong. Taking a deep breath, Iris pulled herself from the negative thoughts, then turned, walking toward the waiting area. It would only take an hour or two.

As she entered the waiting area, she saw Caleb's parents, David, and Rebekah Miller, sitting together. Each was holding a white foam cup of coffee. Iris held her head high, but really, she felt like crawling out of the room. She hadn't considered the Miller's would be there. She should have realized they would be with their son.

"Iris, come. Sit with us," David Miller said when he spotted her in the doorway.

The older couple smiled at her. She didn't know what to expect. Did they know Rose was their granddaughter? Did they harbor feelings of injustice toward her?

Iris looked away as butterflies fluttered in her stomach. She was so nervous to see them, and she knew they must have questions for her. Approaching them, she chose a leather armchair where she could see both of them and judge their reactions.

"How long have you been here?" she asked.

David offered, "About an hour. We came by taxi with Caleb. We'll take him home after."

Iris nodded. She didn't know what to say to them.

"You do not have to be nervous with us. We understand you must have had reasons why you did not tell Caleb about your daughter."

They knew. In some ways, it was a relief to know Caleb told them. Tears filled her eyes. "*Jah*, but I can't get into it here. Maybe someday I can tell you, but not right now. Not today."

Rebekah looked up. Her eyes, dark and warm like her sons, were glittering with unshed tears as well. "Will you let us see her? Introduce us as her mammi and daadi?"

"Of course. I won't keep you apart. Rose needs to know about you and Caleb as well."

"Thank you," Rebekah spoke, her words barely discernible.

"Would you like a refill of coffee?" Iris asked as she stood to get it for the woman. Uncomfortable was an understatement for how she felt. Nerves caused her heart to race, and her breath was quick and shallow. Everything she feared all these years was happening. The difference in her fears was the fact that she now knew Caleb was Rose's father.

She pumped out hot coffee from the air thermos the dietary department kept at each waiting area. Volunteers checked the beverage stations once an hour. If they reported the drinks were running low, the volunteer would go after a coffee cart that held water, tea, coffee, and many packets of beverages.

"Here you go," she said to Rebekah handing the cup to her.

"Sit down, Iris." David's voice was a mere whisper. "We know how hard this is for you and as it is for us, too." He slumped in the chair and crossed his ankles in front of him. "Will you be coming home now?"

Iris shook her head. "I can't. My contract with the hospital isn't up for another couple of months. Besides, I love my job and what I can do to help others. It's difficult to explain, but it is what I've wanted to do since I was a little girl, ever since I saw the vet save the life of a horse my *daed* owned. I knew I wanted to do that for people."

"Very few Amish girls do such things. You are so incredibly young to have such responsibilities. You helped me very much when I came to the hospital. How did you do it?" David asked her.

Laughing softly, Iris shook her head. "I broke all the rules, Mr. Miller."

"Please, just call me David."

"David, it is. Well, when I came out of school, I was only fourteen. I'd been progressed in school a couple of years."

A snort came from Rebekah. "Now, that is not surprising. I saw in you the drive to learn from the time you were little."

"Yes, you're right. I always had library books in my room. My parents had given up on me when it came to reading. I continually brought books home.

I had my cleaning job at the local bed and breakfast, but I never let on that it was only two days a week. See? I broke the rules and lied by omission. My parents trusted me and didn't question my hours. They let me keep the money I made, so no one was the wiser."

"Why do this?" David asked. His brows knitted in a frown.

"I was in the library using the computer to get my GED. Planning that once I passed, I would take college classes online using my work money and a scholarship to pay for it. By the time I was nineteen, I would have a science degree."

"Oh, my," Rebekah sighed. "So, no one knew about this?"

"No, not even Caleb."

David stood and went to the sink, running water into his cup. "What made you leave the Amish, Iris? I always thought it was something between you and Caleb. So now we find out that Rose is our granddaughter? Is this why you left?"

She shook her head. "I didn't know about...about Rose when I left. My father found out about my studies and my deception. Also, he found Caleb and me in the barn, in a, well we..."

"Stop," David said, raising his hand, "we don't need or want to know that part. Go on."

"Anyway, it was a culmination of everything, I suppose. I read online about a school where I could become a Nurse Practitioner. It took me three years to go through it. I watched children in my home that corresponded with my school hours. I could do a lot of it for the first two years online. By that time, Rose was a bit older, and a friend of mine watched her. It worked out well."

"What a story," Rebekah offered. "Your parents. Do they know all about this now?"

Iris stood and paced the floor, her nerves getting to her. The hands of the clock passed slowly. She saw it had only been forty-five minutes since they took Rose back for her procedure. "When I was home to see about my parents testing to do this bone marrow transplant, I didn't have much time to discuss all this with them. They do know that I work at the hospital, but not what my role is. They probably think I clean the place." She smiled with an understanding that the Amish wouldn't think about someone leaving home and becoming a nurse as she had. No, they would feel her inferior and un-Amish in her ways.

"I'm sure when they learn how much you help people, they will be filled with their love for you. Knowing your mother as I do, I know she has never stopped hoping you would come home. You know she misses you, don't you?"

Nodding, Iris offered," I'm sure she does, but how does a person explain in a manner not to hurt others with their decisions. I had to do this. I just had to."

Dr. Rimmell walked into the room smiling.

Iris jumped from her chair and rushed up to him. "How did it go? Is it over?

The doctor took Iris's arm and walked her back to the chair, and then he pulled out a table chair and joined them.

"The procedure was textbook perfect. I feel both of my patients will do fine over the next few months. Rose will take longer, as you know. She has to rebuild her blood cells, and then her immune system has to recover, but she is young."

When the doctor left them, they stood, gathered together to wrap their arms around each other and cried with relief."

"Where's her face?" Rose asked when Rebekah Miller gave her the gift of an Amish doll.

Tears filled Rebekah's eyes, and she swiped at them with a handkerchief she pulled from behind her black apron.

"*Ach*, *Gott* tells us we are all similar to him. So, your baby has any face only you can imagine."

Rose smiled and touched the smooth contour of the faceless doll. "She is beautiful like my mommy."

David squatted down to Rose's level on the floor. "Would you like to sit in a chair so we can talk to you? We must look like giants from your point of view."

Rose raised her arms in the universal symbol of children who wanted someone to pick them up. David reached out and grasped her under her arms and pulled her up and into his. "You are just a mite of a thing. You don't weigh very much."

Rose wrapped her arms around her grandfather and held tight. When David sat in the large wooden rocker in the corner, she stayed latched to him. She squirmed about getting comfortable on his lap as if she had always belonged there.

"Would you look at that?" Rebekah said. "I believe she has stolen her dawdi's heart."

"You are right, *maem*."

From behind them, standing in the doorway, was Caleb. He had come after all.

Rose saw him and asked, "Are you my daddy?"

CHAPTER THIRTEEN

Caleb's breath caught in his chest when Rose saw him standing there. He nodded at her words, not finding his own. Stepping around Iris and his *maem*, he walked toward Rose. His rapid heartbeat played a staccato in his ears. He had to meet his daughter. If only he had known about her earlier. If only...

"*Jah* Rose, I'm your *daed*."

She extended her tiny, little girl hand toward him, and he stared at her welcome.

"You talk like grandma and grandpa."

They all laughed at Rose's words.

Rose slid down David's legs and stood. "This is how we greet strangers, right, mom?" Iris took a few steps forward and extended her hand to Caleb.

"That's right, honey. We do."

Caleb smiled weakly at Iris as if uncertain if she wanted him to reciprocate or not. Iris nodded, then he took Rose's hand. "Wie geht's."

"Hey," Rose said, her voice loud. "Where are you guys from, anyway? You look funny and talk funny, too!"

Caleb burst out laughing. What a precocious child he had. Getting to know her would be a lovely experience. "Ack, we only live a short way from you in a town named Paradise Wells. We will take you there sometime. Would you like that?

Rose nodded slowly. "If it's close, then why haven't I met you before now?"

He snapped his head in Iris's direction. There was no way he could answer without upsetting Rose or her mother.

"We've all been busy, sweetie, but things are calming down for us all, now. We can be together more."

Iris's words satisfied the girl at the moment.

"When you are better, we'll have you out to our farm," David said.

Rose turned, walked toward her grandpa, and crawled back in his lap.

"A real farm, with animals? When can we go there, mom?"

"Soon. You'll be out of the hospital by next week."

Rose's blue eyes lit with a fire behind her wide-eyed gaze. "I will?"

Iris nodded, and she began to cry. Rushing to her daughter, she hugged her where she sat in her Dawdi's lap.

Iris kept crying, and she rushed out the door to the hallway.

Caleb followed her. Was there something about Rose's health that she hadn't told him? Was she still dying?

"Iris," he said as he flew through the door and went to her side. She was sobbing now. With her back to the wall, she slid slowly to the floor.

Caleb knelt in front of her. His heart was doing a rat-a-tat-tat behind his breastbone. The words, no, no, no, screamed through his mind. At this second, he had no doubt he still loved Iris. Now, possibly more than he had at nineteen.

He tried to push the rush of love out of himself, but it didn't work. Sighing slightly, he said, "What is it, liebchen?"

Taking in a shaking breath, she asked, "You used to call me my love all the time. I'm afraid..." A sob sprang from her chest, and she began crying again.

Maem opened the door and came out to see what was happening. "Caleb, what is wrong with her?"

He shook his head to show he had no clue.

Rebekah offered her hand to Iris, and she stood. The sobs were calming from the woman's loving touch. "Kum, we'll talk in the..." she looked down the hallway. "I saw a sign saying family room. Shall we go there?"

Iris nodded. Caleb's *maem* took her by the elbow, and they began to walk away from him.

"Wait for me."

Maem turned and shook her head and motioned for him to get back.

Caleb stood watching for a moment, then returned to his daughter. If she asked where her *maem* was, he'd just tell her she went for *kaffe* to give her new family time together.

In the family room, a counter spread across one wall with hot pots of coffee, decaf, hot water, and hot chocolate. Rebekah went to the offerings and pumped out coffee. "Do you put anything in it, Iris?"

"No, just black, thank you."

The woman got one for herself and joined Iris at the table near a window. The sun shone in, but it had no warmth in it. The sun-blocking properties of the glass prevented it. All the hospital rooms had a strange chill because of it.

Rebekah settled into the chair and took a sip of the steaming beverage. She looked up at Iris and said, "I am so sorry our visiting Rose has upset you, dear."

Iris shook her head, her eyes wide with surprise. She felt awful having given the Miller's the impression their visit had left her emotions in ruin.

"Oh no, Mrs. Miller, that isn't why I'm upset. I am thrilled you all are here to see Rose." Her words came out as a mere whisper. She could barely speak after the crying spell. It had tightened her throat, making her words rough.

The older woman's brows knit with concern. "Has Rose taken a turn for the worse?" She reached across and laid her hand upon Iris's.

Iris bit her lip. What a terrible impression she had given the Miller family. She hadn't meant to break down. With a gusting sigh, Iris said, "It's nothing like that. Rose is doing so well that she can go home next week. And there lies the problem."

Rebekah frowned. "I do not understand why that is a difficulty."

Iris reached up and tightened the elastic around her ponytail, which had loosened. "You see," she said, and once again, tears started pouring down her cheeks. "Rose can't go to daycare because the other children are harbingers of germs and viruses. She can't be around that with her immune system still so low. It will be at least six months before she has recovered enough to go back to her normal routine. Also, the daycare here at the hospital is out of the question with the same concerns."

They sat there quietly for a few beats, then Rebekah said, "Can you stay home with her?"

Iris reached into her pocket for a tissue. Over the past year, they were her constant companion. She patted the tears from her face. "I would do just that if I could, but I can't. I have a contract with the hospital, and also, if I could get out of it, I wouldn't have money for the apartment, no food, and no insurance to cover the cost of Rose's treatments.

"*Ach*! What a dilemma. I see now why you are so upset. Will you wait here for me? I need to do something."

"Sure. I'll have another cup of coffee until you return."

About fifteen minutes later, both Rebekah and David came into the family room. Their faces were shining, and their eyes were sparkling.

"We have some good news for you, Iris, or should I say, we hope you find it is good news."

She heard their words, but the feeling didn't reach her heart. Great news wasn't plentiful in her world. The thought pulled guilt from her soul. Of course, there was goodness. Rose was going to live. That was the best possible outcome. Now, if only she could find a way to support her daughter.

Raising her head, she swiped away the tears and smiled at the couple. Their faces virtually glowed with happiness.

David sat at one side of her, and Rebekah sat on the other. Each was taking her hand in theirs, Rebekah squeezed lovingly. "Iris. We have a plan, and if you agree, it will solve all your problems."

She snapped her head toward Rebekah. "What?"

"Rose can stay with us during her recovery. We have no children at our home, and I have all the time in the world to give our granddaughter. Will you accept our help?"

Iris couldn't grasp a thought as so many ran through her mind. Caleb would be there. What if this family became too close to Rose and wanted to keep her with them? What if they forced her daughter in the Amish ways and confused her? What if...?

But enough of this searching. Iris had to say something. Honestly, this was the only solution to the problem.

"I thank you for your wonderful offer, but..."

"Do you not accept this, Iris?" Caleb asked.

The man stood behind her. His words brought with them a feeling of freezing shards of ice to her heart, and she shivered. It was clear to her now that Caleb hated her.

"I don't know what to say at the moment. It's so sudden. Can I think about it a few days?"

Caleb rounded the sofa where she sat with his parents. He dragged a small chair up as he joined the group. "I do not think waiting is advisable. The doctor wants to release Rose in two days. That doesn't give us very much time to redd up a room for her at the house."

Iris saw she had little recourse but to let her daughter go with her father's family. "I'm worried Rose will be frightened without me at a stranger's home. Also, I wouldn't see her every day. We've been through so much..." she trailed off.

Rebekah lovingly took both of her hands and whispered, "This is for you as well, child. You look exhausted. If we care for Rose, this could ease your mind to where you can get some rest."

"*Jah*, you are welcome to spend your free days with us in Paradise Wells," David spoke softly. "We'll put a bed for you in Rose's room. You can stay with your daughter when you come."

The couple was so gracious with their offer. How could she turn it down?

"Do you agree to our plan, Iris?" Caleb asked.

She nodded then said, "If it won't put you out. Rose can be quite rambunctious when she's feeling well. And there's homeschooling I do with her. She hasn't been well enough to sit all day in a classroom."

David offered, "You will show us this home school method you use, and we'll continue with your guidance, *Jah*."

Iris finally smiled as peace reached her heart. This couple was beautiful. "Yes, I'll bring her work when I come on my days off. I get it from her school. I can enter her grades on my computer when I get home, so the school system has them as well."

Caleb stood, then crossed his muscular arms across his chest. "It's settled then. Will you speak to her doctor and let me know what time to pick her up? I'll give you my cell phone number. We'll be ready for her that way."

A cell phone. That was different for an Amish man.

He reached out his hand. "I'll put my number in your phone if you hand it to me."

What was he so testy about, she wondered? Every time she saw him, he appeared colder than the time before.

Iris reached at her side for her purse, withdrew the phone in its tooled leather case, and offered it to him.

Flipping open the cover, Caleb had his number added within seconds. He sure knew his way around this technology. "*Maem, daed*, let's go tell Rose goodbye."

"Wait a minute! I haven't said I agreed to have you pick up Rose. It would be better if I brought her. I don't want her upset." To say she was annoyed with Caleb and his pushy ways was an understatement.

Rebekah said, "That is the best way, dear." She looked up at her son with a frown. "You have a long way to go learning to be a father, Caleb. That poor little girl would feel you were tearing her away from her *maem*."

Caleb's face reddened, but all he said was, "sorry."

Iris stood and followed the group down the hallway. "I want to be the one to tell Rose of our plans. I think she'll accept it better coming from me."

Not turning around, Caleb muttered icily, "I have no problem with that,"

Caleb's attitude ground up her spine. He had no problem with it. Well, she was Rose's mother. Where did he get off acting so superior and rigid? Where had the sweet boy gone? The one she had loved from their school days. She couldn't find him inside this tall, muscular man. Iris feared it was her fault he'd become bitter.

After the Miller's left, Rose fell asleep from all the excitement, so Iris would have to give her daughter the news tomorrow. She trudged from the room to go to Dr. Rimmell's office and tell him of the new plans.

The doctor was delighted as everyone else was. Too bad she couldn't feel the joy.

"I can leave in one more sleep?" Rose shouted the question with excitement. She grabbed the Amish doll her grandmother made for her and pulled it to her chest. "I get to go home! Oh, mommy!"

Iris's stomach knotted. It was now or never. She had to tell Rose about the plan. Hopefully, Rose wouldn't be too disappointed to learn she was leaving the hospital but not returning to her old way of life.

"Settle down, honey. I have some things to tell you."

Concern pulled at the skin between the little girl's eyes. The poor girl had lived through so many disappointments over the past year. Iris's reluctance to give her child the news held her silent for a moment.

"Mommy! What?" Rose's bottom lip stuck out in a pout.

Taking a calming breath, she began. "You are going out to your grandparent's home for your recovery."

"I am?" Excitement lit the child's eyes.

Could it be possible that she was the only one with the problem of being separated from Rose?

"I'll pack the car with your things, and tomorrow we'll leave for the country. Please try not to be disappointed, but you won't be able to bring your tablet with you, though. The Miller's don't have electricity."

Her baby's eyes rounded in surprise.

"They don't? How does the TV work? And the lights?"

Iris couldn't help but chuckle. "You won't notice the lack of power once you are there for a while."

"I'll miss my tablet and TV, though." Again, her bottom lip protruded in a pout. "But mammi said they have a dog, a cow, and some horses. Do you think they will let me ride the horse?"

"I don't know about that. Usually, the horse is for pulling a buggy. You've seen the black buggies. Remember when we went to the country for my friend Johanna's wedding?"

"Kinda, but I was little then."

"Like you're big now?"

Rose grabbed her hand and kissed the back of it. "I love you, mommy. I can't wait for us to move."

Iris clicked her tongue against her teeth, making a snapping noise. "Uh, about that, sweetie. You see, I have to stay here to work for a while.

That's why you are staying at your grandparent's house. I'll come and spend my days off with you, though."

"Mom! No! I want you there with me." Rose began crying in earnest.

"It will be ok, I promise. You'll have so much fun you won't even notice I'm not there." Iris took Rose in her arms and rubbed her back warmly. "Then, on my days off, I will come and be with you. You'll see that it will all work out. Your stay won't last forever, just while you get stronger. You don't want to be sick again and have to come back to the hospital, do you?"

"I know, mommy, but I'll miss you so much."

"I'll miss you too, sweetheart, but we're strong ladies, aren't we?"

Rose posed with her arms up at shoulder height and made fists to show imaginary muscles. "We are the best!" Then she threw herself back into Iris's embrace.

CHAPTER FOURTEEN

Saturday was Iris's next day off work. The thrill of pushing Rose out the door and to her car was a thrill. Rose bounced in the wheelchair when she spotted their car.

"I'm getting out of here, aren't I, mommy? This is for real."

Iris's heart swelled at her daughter's excitement. The last year had been hell on earth and even worse for Rose.

"I have a suitcase of clothes and some of your toys you picked out the other day to take to your grandparent's house." Iris buckled up the little girl in her protective booster seat in the second seat, gave her a bottle of water for the trip, then slammed the door shut.

She took a deep breath. Butterflies played in her stomach at the thought of going back to the Amish community. Of course, the Miller place was quite a distance from where her parents lived.

Iris's parents hadn't met Rose. Yet. They would be at the Miller's to greet her. Swallowing hard, she wondered how her father would act. When she had told *maem* and *daed* where Rose would stay for her recovery, they had taken it very well. They understood there were fewer people and thus less exposure to viruses at the Miller's.

David and Rebekah were open and loving, having invited her parents to visit whenever they wanted. Was this the beginning of some semblance of restoring her life with her parents? She hadn't been baptized when she left the community; thus, the district hadn't shunned her. Although, the people didn't look favorably at her decisions.

They had been traveling for no more than thirty minutes when Rose began asking if they were getting close yet. Iris laughed under her breath. She supposed every child asked that question of their parents.

When riding in the buggy when she was little, she had to travel what felt like many miles into Paradise Wells.

She smiled and answered, "Not even halfway yet, sweet one. Can you close your eyes and take a short nap? That will make the trip seem as if it's quicker.

"Nope. I want to see everything. I missed a lot staying in the hospital."

Iris's heart pulled at her daughter's words. Rose hadn't left her hospital room very much. She'd gone down to various floors for tests, but outdoors, not so much. One hallway had floor-to-ceiling windows, and Rose loved to look outside to the gardens of flowers. She hadn't been allowed to tarry due to her condition, but Rose loved the journey.

As she drove, memories of her younger years passed through her mind. As much as she wished to push them away, they kept coming at her and, along with them, the emotions she felt at the time. Shockingly, she realized she missed her home. She missed the simplicity of her Amish life but missing Caleb the most dreadful feeling.

She always wanted to help people; that's why she upped her studies to become a nurse practitioner but never expected to face some of the cases that met her in ER.

"Mommy! Look! I see horses." Rose's words pulled her from the deep thoughts assaulting her.

Iris looked in the rear-view mirror and took in her daughter's wide blue eyes. Her baby was excited. The beginning of this little girl's experiences in the Amish world brought so much happiness to her, and Rose's enthusiasm brought on her own.

Iris turned her car onto a crushed gravel road and slowly drove to the Miller home. Her parent's buggy stood near the barn. They didn't have the same horse as when she left. She'd have to ask them if Pepper retired or died.

She heard the clicking of metal against metal and knew Rose had unhooked herself from her car seat. "We're here!" she cried and slid forward. She stood on the car floor to wrap her arms around Iris's neck. "I love you, mommy." The sincerity of her love brought tears to her eyes. It would be challenging to leave Rose here and go back to the city and her job at the hospital.

Iris clicked the button on the door to unlock the childproof lock, then she opened her door, stepped to the back door, and let Rose out. Like un-caging a wild animal, the girl started bouncing with excitement and pent-up nerves.

The mudroom door opened, and Rebekah Miller stepped out and walked down the three wooden steps. The back of the house looked as she remembered. Nothing much had changed.

"Willcumme Rose and Iris. Come in the house. It is cold out here.

Leaving their coats and Rose's items in the car, they rushed inside. Here her parents stood in the kitchen, watching. Their tentative smiles reached their eyes with sincerity.

"Rose," Iris whispered. "These people are my *maem* and *daed*, your other grandparents."

Rose stood there, her mouth partially open for a second, then she said, "So many people. I didn't know about them."

Before Iris's face could bloom red at her daughter's comment, Caleb walked in from the house's living area. "Well, if it isn't my girl, Rose. I'm so happy to see you here. You still remember me, don't you?"

His gaze held a questioning look as he peered at Iris. She knew he was asking if she'd continued to work with Rose that he was her father. Nearly invisible to the people surrounding her, she nodded in affirmation.

Rose turned and looked at her. "Go ahead, give your *daed* a hug."

The little girl took a couple of steps toward him, then looked up and said, "I'm Rose King, and I am your kid. You still remember me, don't you?"

At first, Iris heard chuckles, and then they became ruckus, high-spirited laughter. Rose broke the ice for all of them.

"Of course, I do. We met a couple of weeks ago when you were in the hospital."

Rose's full, pink lips split into a smile. "I remember. I was afraid you forgot me. You didn't come back to see me."

Caleb's eyes darted away from Rose. "I'll get your things from the car and take them to your room." Then he said to Rose, "Do you want to come with me?"

She shook her head. "No."

Caleb raised his eyebrows in surprise.

"I'd go with you," Rose spoke up, but my coat is in the car, and I'd freeze waiting for you, but you can take me to my room when you come back in."

A surge of relief surged through Iris. At first, she felt as if Rose was rejecting Caleb. When she realized it was only her daughter's matter-of-fact way of response, she relaxed.

Caleb walked from the room and out the door to the car.

Rebekah had dinner cooking on the propane stove, which smelled like a hearty stew, and Iris detected a freshly baked bread aroma lingering as well. The bouquets tossed her back into memories of her childhood. Being in the Amish world filled her with homesickness. She hadn't expected this to happen. Her heart felt as if it were being pulled apart. On one side, her joy with her profession, and on the other, her soul cried out for her old way of life. Her closeness to *Gott* lacked in her Englisch life. Sure, she prayed, but she hadn't relied on *Gott* for a long time.

"Once Caleb and Rose come down, we can eat. I'm sure he needs to get back to work. He has orders to get out. A delivery van is coming early next week to take furniture across the country. The Englischer's ordered it from his new website."

Caleb and Rose walked into the room.

"I had no clue you used technology in your business," Iris said.

"*Jah*, Bishop Eischler has been very generous to us and others in the district who were having problems finding customers. He says we must make a living as long as we don't bring it into our home. He and the others in the district have no problem with it."

David piped up. "Now that the doctor has found I do not have Parkinson's disease and has me on some pills for what really ails me, I can be more helpful to Caleb."

"*Jah*, *daed*, and a good help you are. We are giving up our shop in town and keeping the business out here at the farm. *daed* even hired a worker to keep up the farm for our family needs."

"They will spend more time getting to know our Rose," Rebekah offered, then patted the scarf on Rose's head.

"Our business has moved from local to countrywide with the website. A new man came to town to be near his brother, David Fisher. I think he and his family moved here after you left, Iris, but surely you remember Ruby Troyer. She married David."

"Oh my! Yes. I remember Ruby and her son Matthew."

"Matthew married David Fisher's daughter, and they run the farm stay, now."

"When you live here, you feel nothing ever changes, but step out of the snow globe which encompasses your life and look back in, and you find everything has changed as well."

"Anyway, Isaac Fisher is a woodworker as well, and he's interested in buying the building where I have our business showrooms. I think he wants it near the bakery where a newly Amish woman works and lives.

Iris smiled at David. Gossip sure hadn't changed in the district either.

After dinner, her parents sat with Rose in the front room. She listened to them as they told her about the farm and her uncles. They assured Rose, as soon as her doctor okayed it, she could come to their farm and meet the boys.

With the warmth of the fire, both Iris and Rose became sleepy. Caleb entered the room and smiled as he watched Rose drop off to sleep. "Both of you girls should take a nap. I'll carry Rose up to your room if you want to follow.

Iris nodded. They woke early to get on the road. The Miller's assured her that she was welcome to stay with Rose and also, she was welcome on her days off. Iris planned to do just that.

As Caleb picked up Rose from the couch, she snuggled right into his arms. Iris took in his soft, loving smile. Caleb would be a wonderful father for Rose while she was here. But what would happen in a few months when they returned home to the Englisch world? Would he come to visit her? Or would he go and get her on weekends when school was on? Indeed, something would work out.

CHAPTER FIFTEEN

Iris dreaded leaving. She'd never been far away from her daughter. She knew the Miller's would take great care of her, but thoughts of emptiness squeezed tears at the corners of her eyes.

Rose was in the kitchen eating dinner with her new family as Iris toted her bag down the stairs. She stopped in the doorway to the kitchen and just watched their interactions. What she saw caused her to feel like an outcast. The four of them interacted and appeared as a family, not as if Rose was new in their life.

Taking a calming breath, she walked into the kitchen.

"Are you sure you won't eat dinner with us, dear?" Rebekah asked.

Iris shook her head. "No, I'd like to get a head start on the traffic. Going into the city on the Interstate gets terrible in the late afternoon. All those people are heading home after their weekend away."

"We want you to stay for a bit longer. Do you have time for a cup of *kaffe* with us before you go?" David spoke up. He turned to Rose. "Isn't that right, *schnuckiputz*?"

Iris and Caleb both laughed at the word.

"Are you laughing at me?" Rose snorted and crossed her arms in front of her chest. Her bottom lip protruded in a pout.

"It means sweetie pie, you know. I like being dawdi's *putz*."

With those words, everyone laughed and couldn't stop. The young girl smiled even though she didn't know what they were laughing about.

Iris followed Caleb out to her car. He put her suitcase in the back seat, slammed the door, and turned to her.

"Why don't you bring some items to keep here with you when next you come. That way you'll have to carry less.

His eyes were soft and kind, reminding her of the young Caleb she had fallen in love with years ago. "That's a good suggestion," she said as she opened the door. "Please take care of Rose. She is all I have, and I love her dearly."

He reached out and tucked a stray lock of hair behind her ear. He was so close she could smell the wood smoke and fresh-cut lumber that lingered around him. Her heart squeezed in the old familiar way it had when she was eighteen. Did she detect a melting of his icy exterior?

"Of course, I will, Iris. She is mine as well."

His words broke the spell he cast around her. She must come to her senses. There was nothing that could happen between them. She had her life in the Englisch's big world, and he was firmly rooted in the Amish way.

Stepping into the car, she slid under the steering wheel. "I'll see you on my next days off. I'll bring more schoolwork and take the pages I left with her this weekend."

"Safe travels," Caleb said and closed the car door.

Iris turned around in the wide-open area in front of the barn, then drove the gravel lane toward the highway. Tears filled her eyes as she drove away. The next few months were going to be difficult.

CHAPTER SIXTEEN

Iris paced the radiant floor in front of the nurse's desk in the ER. Today was supposed to be her day off, but there was no way she could leave Lancaster. A blizzard hit the area hard, and all the roads were closed. She filled in for other staff members as they were unable to get to the hospital themselves. She had been working for twelve hours now, and it didn't look like she would have a break soon. Numerous injured patients from a car wreck had filled the ER bays. They all worked as quickly as possible to get patients into rooms to make space for others coming in.

They had word that a three-car wreck was bringing in seven people. At any moment, the injured would arrive, and triage started. They would put the worst hurt into a cubicle, and the others treated in a wide-open space at the end of the ER.

The glass doors burst open, and paramedics rushed in with gurneys. Iris directed them into the first empty bay as the first injured in the door usually meant this was the person with the highest trauma level. Triage started when the ambulances arrived at the scene.

Iris rushed into her patient. The paramedics told her it was a fifty-two-year-old man who had head injuries and a broken shoulder and arm.

Quickly Iris ran through her protocols.

When the man became more stable and ready to be sent for a CT scan, she looked at him and realized she'd been working on Eddie Vogel. She was reasonably sure she hadn't seen anyone brought in dressed in the Amish way, so she hoped he hadn't wrecked with Amish passengers.

But seeing someone familiar to her home brought her back down from the rushing high of stabilizing the wounded. She hustled over and helped work on a ten-year-old girl who had lacerations from flying glass and the girl's mother who had a broken leg.

An hour later, a young intern spoke a message to her. "Iris. A man in two wants to see you."

Eddie.

She stepped around the privacy curtain and stood at the end of the bed, holding Eddie while a doctor and nurse worked on him; Iris announced her presence.

"Iris, could you get word to my wife that I'm here and ok? I don't want her to worry."

The nurse patted his hand. "Mr. Vogel, that's been taken care of while you were in CT. Iris took good care of you."

Eddie looked at her then, and his eyes were softer looking than she had ever seen them. "Thank you for all you've done for me today. If you ever need a ride, it's free. For life."

"We'll talk about this later. Right now, I think you're ready to move to your room."

She watched them move him as the cleaning staff took his place and began the clean-up before someone took his place.

The wreck would change all these lives in some way. The Amish would be more fearful of travel, and the others would have fears that showed up in some other way. Her heart went out to them.

At the end of her contract, Iris knew deep down that she had to get out of ER and do some other type of work at the hospital. The continual weight of trauma was getting her down. She wanted to make people better and return them to their daily lives healthy.

Four hours passed without her realizing it. She'd been working continually for sixteen hours, and her body felt it. Turning to Samantha Lodge, the lead nurse on the unit today, she told the woman she was taking a break in the staff room. A short nap would help her focus and be a help in ER and not a detriment. If she were too exhausted, she could make a mistake, and ER staff could cause tragic results.

She walked around the central desk and went into the lounge behind the area. A juice dispenser and a coffee maker sat on the counter. She chose orange juice. The cold liquid refreshed her, and the natural sugar replenished her lagging energy.

The long couch in the middle of the room beckoned to her. Someone had donated throws and pillows, and they looked inviting. Iris realized she felt cold from the fatigue, and she sat and drew a cover over her shoulders. The warmth and comfort tugged her eyelids closed, and soon, she was fast asleep.

When she awoke, three hours had passed. Why didn't anyone awaken her? Indeed, they needed her on the floor.

Brushing her fingers through her tangled curls, she tried to come fully awake. It took a bit, but she was out on the floor within ten minutes talking to a new charge nurse who had come on while she slept.

The ER became quiet, and the snow stopped falling.

"Iris, you live within walking distance, don't you? You should go home and get some rest. We'll do ok here."

She nodded. "Yes. Just around the corner. Are you sure I should go?"

"Absolutely. Two more nurses are on their way now that machinery and manpower are out working on the roads. Go home and enjoy your days off. You deserve it."

Iris nodded. "I need it. I'm exhausted."

She went back to the staff lounge and to a room near it where her locker was. She gathered her coat and boots and headed home to her empty apartment. At this moment, she felt so empty and alone. She was glad her baby was recovering, but the distance and the weather didn't make it easy.

Her days off were nonexistent. The snow kept coming, and the patients followed the storms to the ER. Each time she called Caleb, she could hear a distance in his voice.

Iris arrived at the Miller place early Saturday morning. It was her first day off in two weeks. She was so excited to see Rose that she hurried out of town and forgotten to pick up Rose's schoolwork. Her shoulders sagged, not only from not remembering the schoolwork but also from fatigue. It all struck her at once. What kind of mother was she?

As she turned off the car, Caleb, with Rose close behind him, jogged toward her. Quickly, opening the car door, she stepped out. Then, she swallowed hard and stared at her daughter. Rose was dressed Amish. A glistening white apron covered her long blue dress, and a *kapp* covered her red hair.

"*Maem*! I'm so glad you're finally here!" Rose rushed into her arms.

Iris wrapped her arms around her daughter, hugging her tightly. The girl had more body covering her bones. "I've missed you too, sweet one." Once they parted, Iris pushed Rose away from her a bit. "Back up. Let me see you."

The aroma of freshly baked bread in the overly warm mudroom cocooned her in feelings of homesickness. She was raised like this, and each time she came back into the Amish world, the more she felt like a deserter. After talking to her parents many times since she'd returned to the district, she realized just how much she loved her parents and treasured the community of Paradise Wells.

"Let's go inside. It's freezing out here." Caleb said as he stamped his feet against the ground to move the blood to his freezing feet. "I'll get your bag and meet you two inside."

Iris wrapped her wool cape around Rose, and they rushed toward the house and up the wooden steps. The mudroom door creaked as it opened, which was a familiar sound to Rose as she had come to the Miller's door so many times over her life. The thought brought a wave of sinking sadness through her mind. The more she was away from her Amish community, the deeper her desolation.

Entering the kitchen, she found Rebekah finishing the breakfast dishes. "Have you had breakfast, Iris?" she asked over her shoulder. "I saved a few pancakes for you."

The sound of warm food made a big smile pull across her face.

"Please, mommy, I'll sit with you."

"And eat a few bites of your own as well," Rebekah said, laughter filling her voice as well as the words. "Iris, this girl eats more than she weighs every day."

She sat at the table, and Rose crawled onto her lap. "Your care for her shows. Look how she's changed over the past two weeks."

The sound of Caleb's shoes on the stairs took her attention. He nearly slid into the kitchen in his haste.

"Calm down, son," Rebekah said. "You have plenty of time to talk to Iris."

Iris frowned as she looked at the man. "Is there a problem? You look a bit concerned."

"*Jah*, for sure and certain. I have a problem with your schedule."

"Enough, Caleb. There is a time and place for your conversation, and now is not the time." She frowned and looked down at her granddaughter. "Here are your cakes. Enjoy them...girls." She placed the plate in front of Iris and patted Rose's head.

"I see we have butter, honey, and jam. What do you think I want on the cakes?" Iris asked Rose.

"Honey, mom! Why haven't we ever had honey before? I love it."

Iris shook her head. Rose bloomed living here with the Miller's. A sinking feeling of gloominess surrounded her as everyone around the table focused on Rose. The youngster was the center of their lives. She wasn't sure when this happened, but it took place right in front of her.

Rose and she became a team from the moment the baby was born. Together forever. Or until more family entered her daughter's life. As they ate, Rose talked about books, food, and plants. Iris couldn't focus on the subjects. Her only thoughts were of losing her daughter. Right now, she wanted to scoop up her baby and dash for her car, never to show up on the Miller's step again.

"Iris," Caleb said.

Her attention snapped to him. "I-I'm sorry. The drive was harrowing today, and I'm exhausted from the past couple of weeks with no days off." She pushed her plate away and then wove her fingers through the large coffee mug handle. She took a sip of the warm liquid and relaxed. What had she been thinking? The Miller's weren't trying to keep Rose from her. She was doing the job herself.

"Would you like to take a sleigh ride with me before the storm closes in?"

"Daed! Daed! Can I go too?" Rose cried excitedly and jumped up from her chair, and rushed to his side. "Pleeeease?"

He shook his head but wrapped an arm around her shoulders to give her the unwanted words. "No, sweetie, this ride will be for you, mommy, and me. She needs to have a relaxing sled trip."

"Okay," Rose whispered dejectedly under her breath. "I guess that's ok. Will you be back soon?"

Iris patted her daughter's hand and said, "Of course, we will. You know how easily I become cold." She shivered to act out the sensation.

Caleb tipped his head toward her and smiled softly. He so reminded her of their youth when he had played pranks on her in school. "You don't need to look at me like that. I meet your challenge for a ride in the snow."

He stood, reaching his hand out to her. "Then let's do it before it gets any worse."

Fifteen minutes later, they were in the sleigh. Caleb wore a thick coat, and he had wrapped Iris in a heavy quilt clear over her head, around her shoulders, and down around her feet.

As the horse took off with a jolt, she laughed for a long time. Happiness through Rose's illness was scarce. Now, she had everything to be happy about. Rose was in remission, and the doctor told her there was no reason to believe that would change. They must wait it out for Rose's immune system to gather steam protecting her from illnesses.

As they glided along over the thick snow, the world around wrapped them in silence. Even the horse hooves made little sound in the snow.

Caleb turned to a copse of trees. If she correctly remembered, the opening between the trees led to the wide creek where, in her childhood years, she and all her friends ice-skated.

Iris turned toward Caleb. "Why are we coming out here? Surely, we aren't skating today. The snow will have covered the ice."

"*Jah*, it would. But remember how the trees made a canopy and where we made the bonfire to keep warm?

She nodded and narrowed her eyes at him questionably.

"We are stopping there for a bit. I want to talk to you without little ears, nor my parents as well."

His statement seemed to freeze her heart as if mocking her cold nose. What did he want to say in private? Her pulse erratically bumped along. This didn't feel right. If it were, he wouldn't have minded speaking in front of Rose and the Miller's.

Pulling the horse and sled under the canopy of tree branches, they stopped. Iris anxiously waited for him to speak. His Adam's apple under his scarf bounced up and down as he swallowed.

If Caleb couldn't form the words, she was facing something terrible.

Finally, after waiting for what seemed several minutes, she spoke up.

"For heaven's sake, Caleb. What is it? What do you have to tell me?

He had been gazing at the blanket covering her legs, but he now glanced up. "This isn't easy to say, Iris, but...I want Rose to stay here permanently.

CHAPTER SEVENTEEN

"You want what?"

"I want her here with us permanently. I don't think living in the city is good for her. Your schedule is too much. How are you going to care for her when you are at work all the time? The only people raising her will be babysitters. At least with us, she will be cared for and with one of us all the time."

Iris was stunned. She hadn't suspected her fears would come to fruition, but they had. "No! You can't mean this! I let you into our lives, and now you want to take over. You cannot have my daughter."

"Our daughter." He whispered the words. "It is the best thing for her."

Iris jerked forward on the bench seat. "No. I'm what's best for her. I am her mother."

Reaching over with his gloved hand, he placed it over the top of her cold skin. "Just think about it, alright? I knew you'd act this way. You have always been hot-headed.

Under the blanket, she crossed her arms over her chest protectively. She felt the sensation Caleb ripped out her soul. "Is that all you have to say?"

"Not really. I'd hoped we could talk about a way to get you to stay here as well. Couldn't you come home and live at your parents' home? We could share Rose that way. It could work. If you allowed it to."

"I can't leave the hospital. I'm under contract."

"For how long?"

She didn't want to tell him that it was only for another month. If he knew that she didn't have a job placement yet, it would just give him more ammo against her. For sure, she didn't want to return to her parents. It would be too difficult.

"How about this," he said, "Take some time to think about it. The next time you come to visit, we can talk some more about you returning to your true home."

She said no more and withdrew into herself. How could Caleb ask her this? Was this reason she'd felt so gloomy at the breakfast table earlier?

Words wouldn't come out as she swallowed past the lump in her throat. Nodding, she swallowed again, and tears began to roll down her cheeks.

"Oh, Iris, please don't cry. I'm only trying to offer a way to give you and Rose a happier life."

Anger bubbled through her, dissolving both her tears and the lump in her throat. "Caleb," she spat, "I don't want your help. You have nothing to fix. I can take care of my daughter fine by myself."

Caleb didn't argue with her, but she saw the muscles in his jaw throbbing. He was angry at her. His back stiffened, and he didn't look at her.

Finally, he spoke, his words flat. "The snow is falling harder, and we'd better get back to the house." Flicking the reins, the horse moved in a slow canter. Thick clouds and falling snow obscured the sun.

As Caleb maneuvered the sleigh across the snow, the wind picked up, and the wall of flakes came at them harder. Iris reached up, knocking off the snow settling on her eyelashes before they could freeze.

"How can you tell where we are? All this snow and wind blind me." A gust of wind pulled her words out into the snow-filled air.

"Nickers knows the way home. We don't have to worry about it." He turned his head and faced her. "Have you forgotten all you knew about this way of life?"

When she shook her head, the quilt slid from her hair. She reached up and pulled it higher and formed a cubbyhole around her head to keep the snow out. "Just get us back, and we can talk about it later."

Caleb flicked the reins, and the horse moved quicker through the onslaught. Lost in her thoughts, she was surprised when they arrived back at the Miller's in short order. He neared the back door and stopped. "Go in. I'll be in the barn taking care of the horse and the sleigh."

Without a word, Iris tightened the quilt around her and slid out. The snow was over the top of her winter boots and fell inside. She shivered, then ran to the back door. She raced inside. The blast of warm air heated by the small wood stove in the mudroom made her think of a comforting wall of thick warmth.

"We are back safely!" she hollered into the kitchen as she stomped the snow from her boots then kicked them off on the rug set against the wall placed there for just this reason.

Her socks were wet, so she took them off and put them over the backs of her boots to dry. Removing the quilt, she was surprised to see Rebekah standing in the doorway. "Here, let me help you with that. I'll hang it near the stove to dry. It seems the quilt kept you dry. Just hang your coat on the hook and meet me in the kitchen."

"It's miserable out there," Iris said, unzipping her puff coat."

"I fixed a pot of hot chocolate for your and Caleb's return. It has been difficult to keep Rose out of it."

Just the sound of her happiness relaxed Iris, and she smiled. Her laughter tinkled across the room to her. "I'm thrilled to have Rose here with you, but Caleb told me on our ride that he wants Rose to stay here. Permanently."

Rebekah looked away from Iris, showing she knew his plans to talk to her during their outing. "You are a mother, Rebekah. How would you feel if someone wanted to take your child from you? That's how it feels to me. He wants your family to keep her forever."

"But Iris..."

"I know. Caleb wants me to stay here, but I cannot do that. I have a successful career that I've worked hard to create. I cannot give it up."

Rebekah poured the hot chocolate into a giant-sized mug, then walked to the table and handed it to her.

"After the contract is up, I don't know what I'm going to do. Rose and I might have to go to a different state or..."

"No!" then loud thumping sounds.

Iris jumped from her chair and raced to the stairway. Rebekah was close to her heels.

Rose lay in a heap at the bottom of the stairs, one leg spayed at an impossible angle, and she was silent. The girl looked so small lying there.

"Rose!" both Iris and Rebekah screamed.

Iris knelt and wiped the red curls from her daughter's face. Her eyes didn't even flutter when she called her name. Touching the side of her throat, Iris felt for a pulse and found it, but it was slow. The girl was unconscious.

"*Maem*, Iris! What's happening? I heard screaming." Caleb rushed to them, skidding to a stop when he saw Rose at the foot of the stairs. "What happened?"

"We're not sure. We heard Rose scream and found her like this."

Iris looked up at him. "I'm sure her leg is broken."

"Can you fix it?" Caleb asked, peering into her eyes.

Shaking her head, she said, "No. We need to get her to the hospital. Now! My car is close to the door. Will you help me carry her out?"

He shook his head. "We can't use your car. The roads are closed. The snow is too deep."

Fear slammed through her. "How are we going to get her help?"

They stood there staring at each other for a moment when Rebekah piped up, "Use the sleigh and take her into doctor Stolfuz's office.

Caleb, use your phone and call ahead to let the doctor know you'll be coming soon."

"Here, you can use my cell phone," Iris spoke and offered the phone with an outstretched hand.

Reluctantly, Rebekah reached for it. "How do you work it, Iris?" she whispered under her breath.

Iris whipped her fingers across the screen, and the phone lit up. She pressed on an area of the screen then asked, "Do you have the number?"

Caleb piped up with it, and Iris entered the number on the phone. She handed the phone to Caleb. He must be acquainted with the doctor to have his phone number memorized.

In just a moment, Caleb was talking. Explaining what had taken place. "*Jah*, I'll get her there on the sleigh just a quick as we can." He handed to phone back to Iris.

"Should we get her straightened out before I go bring the sleigh up?"

"Yes, I'll tell you what to do. We don't want to create more injuries as we move her. She ran her hands over her daughter as she did for her patients in ER. She found only a lump on her forehead, and by the looks of the wall, her head banged into it, causing a shallow dent. Iris sighed with a stroke of relief. At least it wasn't the wood step or newel post.

"I'm going to move her leg into a straighter position. Rebekah, do you have another quilt we can wrap her in?"

The woman didn't say a word but rushed from the hallway, through the living room to her bedroom, and then raced back with the blanket. "Did Caleb go for the sleigh?"

"It's out there already," David spoke behind them. "I heard you in here, came in, and saw what was happening, so I readied the sleigh. I know no one could get to town with all this snow."

Iris smiled at David. He was such a kind man.

"Mommy!" Rose's eyes fluttered open. "I fell, and I got hurt." She began to cry softly.

"You will be ok, schnuckiputz," David said to his granddaughter. "You are going for a ride in the sleigh."

As a bit of a smile pulled at the corners of Rose's mouth. Her eyes fluttered shut, and Iris tapped at Rose's chin. "Waikie, wakie, little one. Stay awake for us. You don't want to miss the sleigh ride."

Rose opened her eyes just as Caleb walked in. "Daddy! I'm broke."

"Your mommy told me your leg is banged up, so we are going to see the doctor."

"In the sleigh, right?"

"Right. Now, I'm going to pick you up and carry you out to the sleigh."

Rose's eyes knit with concern. "Will it hurt?"

He dropped to one knee, looking directly into his daughter's eyes. "I don't know, sweetie, but be strong, ok?"

"Ok."

Caleb picked her up from the floor. Rose didn't make a peep.

The ride took the better part of an hour, and they were covered in a thick blanket of snow when they arrived at Dr. Stolfus' home, where he had a 2-room office. One exam room and a waiting room.

The doctor, white-haired but still attractive, appeared to be in his late sixties, entered from a door she suspected led to his home.

Caleb carried Rose into the waiting area.

"So, who do we have here?" Dr. Stolfus asked.

"I'm Rose, and I'm broken. Can you fix me?"

The doctor neared the little girl in her father's arms. "I think I can. Why don't you all follow me to the exam room, and we'll see what sorts of injuries you have." He ruffled her hair, exposed now because her *kapp* had come off during her tumble down the stairs.

Rose smiled up at him. Creating confidence was the number one thing to carry out when meeting patients and their families for the first time. The man was good at it because Iris felt such a relief placing her daughter in his hands.

Caleb laid his small girl on the long, hard table.

Dr. Stolfus took his stethoscope from a table, placed them in his ears, and listened to Rose's heart and lungs. "You're such a good patient. You weren't afraid at all of me checking you over."

Rose offered. "I've been in the hospital for years and years, so I'm not afraid."

Dr. Stolfus looked at Iris with a questioning look in his eye.

"Rose is in remission from leukemia. Caleb gave her his bone marrow, and she's now on the mend."

"What a brave girl you are, Rose," the doctor said. "Be strong a little while longer while I check your leg. I can see the way it's bent that you broke a bone in it."

Rose nodded and watched him examine her by propping herself up on her forearms.

"So, you want mommy to raise the head of the bed so you can see and be comfortable at the same time?"

She nodded once again, and Iris pressed a button, and the upper part of the exam table raised.

Within minutes, the Dr. rolled a portable x-ray machine into the room. She and Caleb went to the hallway. Now that she wasn't in Rose's presence, tears filled her eyes, and a sob escaped her.

Caleb put his arm around her shoulders and pulled her to him in a comforting hug. Dang, it felt good to her to have his support. He was such a good man, and he would be a wonderful father for Rose.

"I'm sorry to be such a big baby. Rose has been through so much. She sure doesn't need more problems."

"She's a kid, Iris. Things happen to kids."

"Yeah, I know you're right."

Dr. Stolfus opened the door and told them to come back in. He held an iPad in his hands and held it up for all to see. "Rose. You broke your tibia. That's the big bone there." He pulled up a rolling chair nearer his patient. "See it?" he pointed at the picture. "Right here is a crack, and the top part of the bone is off to the side."

Iris sighed.

"Can mommy fix it? She's a doctor, you know."

Dr. Stolfus turned his head and looked at her with narrowed eyes.

"I'm a physician's assistant. I work in ER at General in Lancaster."

"You can help me set her leg then."

Rose sat bolt upright on the exam table. "Is it going to hurt?" She cried. "I don't want it to hurt more."

"I have a little pill you put under your tongue. In just seconds, you will be asleep, and when you wake up, it will be all over."

The girl's eyes drew together in a frown. "Okaaay," the word drawled out. "Mommy, will it work."

Iris leaned over the table and brought her arms around her daughter. "I know you're scared, honey, but I've helped hundreds of children this way myself. I won't let anything happen to you."

Rose's lips quivered into a smile, and she opened her mouth wide in acceptance of the pill.

A few minutes later, Rose slept comfortably. "Would you like help, doctor?" Iris asked.

"This should be a simple fracture reduction." Dr. Stolfus manipulated Rose's leg. "Would you position the x-ray? We'll see how it's lined up."

Iris moved the portable machine and stepped from the room. "Caleb followed her out into the hallway. "Will her pain be bad after this?"

"Not too bad, hopefully. Dr. Stolfus might send home a couple of pain meds to get her through the next few hours, but beyond that, no."

"Come on back, the doctor called. Everything looks good, and we will get her in a cast."

Iris helped the doctor immobilize Rose's leg. They were cleaning up the mess when Rose awoke. "Mommy, is it over?"

"It is, sweetie. Look at your leg."

"Oh! It's bright pink!" Rose cried. "I love it." The girl reached out to Iris, and they came together in a healthy hug.

"Hey, don't I get one, too?" Caleb asked and went to the other side of the table.

Rose looked at him and smiled. "You do *daed*. I love you." She released her hold on Iris and wrapped Caleb in her tiny arms. "You are the bestest sled driver. Are you going to take us back home soon?"

"Yes, as soon as the Dr. says you can leave."

Dr. Stolfus finished washing his hands at the sink. "You can go any time now. I do want to speak to your parents for a minute before you leave. Is that okay with you?"

Rose nodded. When none of the adults moved, she said, "Go on. I want to go home soon." With those words, her bright blue eyes drifted closed.

Across the hall was the Dr.'s office. They went in, and he opened a locked cabinet. He pulled out a large bottle, shook a few pills into a small envelope. After scribbling words on it, he handed them to Iris. "Only use one every twelve hours if you must. None would be better if she can get through it, but don't be afraid to use them."

The doctor gave her the same speech she gave to her parents in ER. She was familiar with the medication.

"I'll drop by sometime tomorrow, or if the roads are still closed, I'll call."

She wrote down her cell number and her mailing address on a pad. "Thank you for everything, Dr. I'm so glad Rose had your gentle care and kindness."

The return trip felt faster this time. Iris was becoming more acquainted with the old Amish ways.

CHAPTER SEVENTEEN

Overnight, the snow stopped falling, and the wind calmed. As Iris lay snuggled in the bed, she heard the sound of machinery in the distance. Probably snowplows. Hopefully, she could return to Lancaster and her job on Monday. The thoughts of leaving were unsettling. At the end of each weekend, it became harder and harder to return to her English life. Now, with Caleb wanting Rose full-time, turmoil swirled through her. What was she going to do?

Rose slept through the night with her casted leg elevated on pillows. It must have stopped hurting after Iris gave her a pain pill. She sat there waiting and watching Rose for any signs of discomfort until they both fell to sleep.

"Mommy. Are you awake?" Rose asked in a whispered voice.

Iris turned on her side to face her daughter. "I am. Good morning to you. How are you feeling?"

Rose giggled. "I don't hurt, but I have to go potty. Do I have to use the crutches?"

"How about I carry you across the hallway? You're not too big for me yet."

Rose pushed herself up in the bed. "I think I need help with this big leg."

Iris tossed back the covers and went to Rose, lifting the casted leg over the side of the bed. "There. Just wrap your arms around my neck, and I'll pick you up."

In just moments, she had Rose in the bathroom, and she stood waiting in the hallway with the closed door behind her.

"I thought you two would sleep longer," Caleb said as he neared her coming from the window end of the hallway. "How is our Rose doing?"

"Fine. She slept through the night and didn't need a pain pill the doctor sent home."

"That's wonderful. Let me know when Rose is ready to come downstairs, and I'll carry her to breakfast."

"Thanks, she's gotten a lot heavier since she's been here with your family."

"It agrees with her," Caleb spoke humbly. He gazed at the floor.

Iris called to Rose, "Are you about done in there?" She wanted to redirect this conversation. Discussing Rose's living situation wasn't something she wanted to do in the hallway. Later, possibly, but not right now.

Breakfast was a long, drawn-out ordeal for Iris. No one said much besides discussing the weather and the shop orders. The elephant in the room was Rose's permanent stay with the Miller family.

A knock at the front door startled them. It had been so quiet during the recent blizzards.

Rebekah went to the door. Iris heard someone come in, and distant voices of Rebekah and a man filtered into the kitchen. Moments later, Dr. Stolfus entered the kitchen.

"Would you like *kaffe*, doctor?" Mrs. Miller asked.

"Jah sounds good."

David pointed to the chair beside Rose and said, "Take a load off, if you will. How is it you were able to make it out here?"

"The snowplows have been out. I was right behind one. The driver was one of my patients since he was a boy. So, when I got to the turn to your place, he just turned in front of me. You'll find most of your road is open. He turned in the large area before coming up the side of the house."

"Awk, we didn't even hear it," Caleb said. I'll have to thank him the next time I run into him.

The doctor looked over at Rose. She was gulping down a big glass of chocolate milk. "How did you do last night, little one? Any problems?"

She shook her head. "Nope. Mommy put my leg up on a big pillow, and I fell to sleep."

Dr. Stolfus peered at Iris. "That right? Any pain pills needed?"

Smiling, Iris offered, "Only one. I have a tough daughter, doctor."

"I guess you do. I came by to check on Rose, but I see you have everything under control. If you don't mind, I'd like to speak with you in private if I could."

Iris got the familiar sinking feeling in the pit of her stomach. She usually felt this way when a doctor asked to talk to her alone. She was trained over the last year to expect the worst.

She saw Caleb looking at her with fear in his eyes as well. He was getting trained as well, it seemed.

"Is it ok if we take our coffee to the living room," the doctor asked Rebekah.

She nodded and said, "It is alright. You two go ahead, and we'll see to it Rose eats all her food."

Iris saw that oatmeal and toast were the stars today when she came down to the breakfast table. Not one of her daughter's favorite things to eat. Her grandmother might have a fight on her hands with that one.

The doctor and Iris each sat in matching overstuffed chairs that faced each other. A coffee table in the middle with crochet coasters placed about the beautiful wood.

"Iris, I know you are formerly Amish and from this community."

She nodded and followed his words, confused. It didn't appear this had anything to do with her daughter.

"I'm sixty-four, and I want to retire. I'm looking for someone to take over my practice."

The words lay on her mind like a thick blanket. What was doctor Stolfus telling her? When she didn't respond in her confusion, the doctor continued. "I called Lancaster General this morning and talked to the doctor that oversees your work. He only has rave reviews for your work. It appears everyone at the hospital loves you."

"Well...thank you, or should I say, thank them." Iris laughed nervously and blushed. Her Amish heritage showed itself as flattery, pride; those things were not of the Amish.

"What I'm trying to get at is this. Would you be interested in taking over my practice here in Paradise Wells?"

Now she understood, but she was even more numb. All she could think of was that this could be her salvation from her job ending at the hospital, the Miller's wanting to take her daughter away. And most of all, bring her back to her Amish roots.

As the words began to sink in, Iris asked the man, "You work from your home, don't you? Last night was a blur when we brought Rose in to see you, but I got the impression it was your home, not a clinic."

"Yes, you're right. We'd have to get you set up somewhere in town and find you a place to stay."

Iris pushed her hands through her red, curly hair. Her scalp was damp with sweat. "Can I think about this? It's so sudden that I'm not thinking clearly...scratch that thought...I'm unable to think at all."

"Yes, of course, but I'd like to have an answer soon. I have patients who will need follow-ups, pregnant women and older folks, and all of them need a breath of time to come to the fact that someone new will be tending to their needs."

Iris stood, offered her hand to the doctor as he hoisted himself up as well. "I have a question for you as well. Will you be the doctor overseeing my work?"

The doctor looked away from her gaze. "I will until we can find someone younger than me. My wife and I want to travel and possibly sell our big home and settle somewhere with a bit more to offer. Possibly a senior community." He turned toward the door.

"Please bid the Miller's goodbye. I see you have Rose's small break under control. Just bring her in, that is, if you aren't the care provider in charge." He chuckled and opened the door, and stepped outside in the bright sunlight, amplified by the mounds of glittering snow.

Iris closed the door and leaned back against it in awe. A job landed in her lap—a position where she could be near her community.

"Did he leave already?" Caleb asked her when he walked into the living room.

"He did."

"What's the matter with you? You look pale. Are you not feeling well?"

Iris walked toward the sofa. "Would you come to sit with me for a moment? I need to talk to you." She pushed back her hair from her face.

He walked to the sofa and sat at the opposite end, and faced Iris where she dropped at the other end. "You're worrying me a bit."

Shaking her head, she said, "Doctor Stolfus asked if I'd be interested in taking over his practice in Paradise Wells."

"*Ach*! That's wonderful. It would solve everything. We could share Rose, and if you had some long hours or something came up, we are here to watch Rose for you. When will you start?"

"Wait a minute. Don't go getting that buggy before the horse. I haven't given him an answer yet. There is a lot to think about."

Caleb frowned and braced his elbows on his knees with his chin in his hands. "What are you so afraid of?"

Iris thought about it for a few beats, then taking in a big gulp of air, she answered, "You."

His eyes widened. "You can't be serious. You are afraid of me? What have I done to make you fear me?"

"Seriously? You don't know? You hate me, that's why."

His head shook slightly, and his cheeks turned red. "That's not true. My feelings are far, far from hatred." He scooted across the sofa and, sitting on the edge, turned to face her. "I love you still." The sound was barely above a whisper.

Iris reached up and moved a lock of auburn hair from near his eye. "I love you too, but it could never work between us. I'm more Englisch than Amish, the community and the Bishop would never accept me back in their good graces. And what about Rose? How would she learn to become Amish?"

A hooted laugh came from him. "Have you seen our daughter recently?" She loves her new Amish-styled clothing, her faceless doll, and she's speaking like us. Within a few months, she will be able to hold conversations with us."

"Caleb, how can you not hate me after the way I kept Rose from you all those years?"

"I've wondered why you did this, but I don't hate you now. You have shared Rose with our family, and it takes a good person to do something like that. But I wish you'd tell me why you did all this to keep us separated."

Iris glanced to the kitchen door.

"They can't hear us, and besides, Rose is keeping them entertained. We have time. Please tell me why all this happened? It's been a mystery to me."

She told him all that led up to her leaving, but her throat tightened when she got to the point of the attack.

"This can go no farther than between you and me. Do you understand?"

Caleb nodded and took a chest-filling breath.

"I had no intentions to leave. Oh, I was so excited to tell our parents we were getting married, but then..."

"What?"

"Coming from the library, I was late, and it was getting dark. Just as I unhitched the horse, I was grabbed by two men and dragged behind the dumpster, and...and...they raped me."

"No. Oh no."

Tears rolled down her cheeks, and she sobbed. Caleb took her in his arms and held her close, and let her cry. "This happened at the same time frame of when we made love in the barn."

She said nothing but bobbed her head.

"Do you know who they were?"

"Not Amish," she got out of her tight throat. "There's more."

I waited until all the lights were out before I went inside to pack, but my *daed* was in the living room. He saw me come in and called to me." She shuddered at the memory.

When he saw my bruises and torn dress, he thought you had done something to me, and he forbid me to have anything to do with you. You know the rest."

"I am so sorry this happened to you."

"Caleb, I don't expect you to forgive me for all of this, especially for the hurt I've caused you. That's why I don't know if it's a good idea to take over the medical clinic." Iris sighed noisily. "I'll have to give this good thought. As it stands, my contract is nearly completed with the hospital, so it makes sense for me to come here, but Caleb, will the people from our district come to me?"

"I think they will. You weren't shunned, after all, because you weren't baptized."

Looking to the floor to avoid Caleb's eyes, she offered, "You know how the people are here. It matter's little. If they feel you don't deserve coming back, they won't acknowledge you."

"You forget one thing. We all stood behind you, and many of us were tested for Rose's transplant. That says a lot to me. I think they will welcome you back."

"I'll speak to Bishop Eischler. Will you take me to him with the sleigh?" She stood. "It's a beginning to come to a decision."

Caleb joined her, took her by the shoulders, and pulled her into an embrace. She felt his warmth, his care, but the word love still pushed her away. Was he encouraging her to take over the medical clinic as a means to be closer to Rose? Somehow, she had to know if he genuinely cared for her or if it was a ruse on his part. A ploy in which he wasn't aware was happening to him.

CHAPTER EIGHTEEN

Nearly a week passed since her stay at the Millers, and she was still uncertain as to what her plans entailed. Caleb took her to the Bishop, and his concern was if she planned to return to the Amish ways or if she planned to keep to her English ways.

Iris knew that answer deep in her heart. She was Amish and always had been. The ways never left her. The only requirement the Bishop had was that she attend the classes and become baptized.

Nothing he asked was complicated. On the cold trip back to the Miller's, Caleb asked her if he could court her.

After explaining why she kept Rose from him, her words appeared to melt the ice surrounding him. At last, she knew where she belonged. Paradise Wells was her home, and Caleb Miller was the love of her life.

Standing in the middle of the ER with machines beeping and people scurrying around, Iris realized she lived with one foot firmly planted in each world. She only had a week to go to fulfill the contract she signed two years ago. HR left her a message to come in following her shift. The day arrived. She'd sign the papers and end this phase of her life. The last thing she would do is call doctor Stolfus when she got home this afternoon and accept his offer to take over the clinic. Iris hoped it was the right thing to do. She had the next two days off, and she was headed to Paradise Wells to see Rose and Caleb. She would meet with the doctor and iron out the transfer of the medical information with the State of Pennsylvania.

Before another thought struck her, the ER's glass entry doors switched open, and a paramedic called out vital information on her next patient.

Now what? Now what? Now what?

The words screamed through Iris' mind on the drive from Lancaster to Paradise Wells. She must talk to Caleb. No way could she focus on anything else but her first and only love. He was the only thing that made sense in her world right now. So much had happened in the past four hours.

Iris didn't realize she'd turned off the interstate miles back. It shook her. She could have wrecked and herself or some other unsuspecting driver. Ahead, the turn off to the Miller's place flashed her awareness into focus. She turned in, navigated the long driveway toward the house, and arrived safely.

Closing her eyes, she sat there unaware until a knock came at the side window. Caleb stood there, his brows knitted together in concern. Tears flowed down her cheeks.

"Open the door!"

His words brought her mind to the surface enough that she pressed the unlock button.

Caleb quickly opened the door and knelt to look at her face-to-face. "What's the matter, liebchen? Are you ok?"

Iris looked at him and broke into sobs.

"Come on, let's go in the house. It's cold out here."

Shaking her head, she whispered, "No. Your family...Rose...they are all in there. Close the door and get in here."

Caleb did as she instructed and softly closed the door.

"Now, tell me what's happening with you. I've never seen you so upset. Is Rose sick again?"

She shook her head then dropped it against her hands at the top of the steering wheel as she wept in earnest.

"Ish lieb you so much," Caleb whispered, "please tell me what's wrong. You can tell me anything." Reaching over the console between them, he rubbed her shoulders.

His touch caused her to cry harder. She didn't think that was possible. They sat there until she had no more tears and her hiccupping sobs dwindled. "I can't get nearer you to hold you, Iris. What can I do to help?"

Iris sniffed, then said, "Can I use your handkerchief?"

Sliding forward on the seat, he reached into his back pocket and pulled out a sparkling white square of cloth, and handed it to her.

She mopped her eyes and nose. Stalling for time, Iris couldn't find the words to tell him. Resting her head on the seat back and closing her eyes helped calm her. She dreaded this moment but knew she had to tell him. What direction should she go? The only word that would come to her was.

Torn.

"Please, Iris, let's talk about this. You are scaring me."

"Oh! I'm not trying to do that to you. I'm just so..." Up cropped that word again. Torn. "I don't know what to do. Doctor Schultz gave me a deadline for my decision. I don't know what to do. The deadline is today!"

Caleb turned in the seat and faced her. "I thought you would have contacted him by now and accepted his offer. That's what you wanted a few days ago."

"It was until a while ago." Her words rang flat and unemotional to herself.

She saw the muscles in Caleb's jaw jumping in agitation. "What changed?" Anger tinged the words.

"Doctor Rimmell, Rose's oncologist, offered me a job as well. I'd work on the oncology floor, and I'd have decent working hours and weekends off. The perfect situation for Rose."

Caleb's face paled, and he looked away from her. "It's not just for Rose, is it?"

She shook her head, and more tears started to fall. "No. It's for me as well. I have worked up to a job like this. It's my career."

"And you'll turn your back on the Amish and me once again." Caleb opened the door and slid out. "I'm going to the barn. Go ahead and gather Rose's possessions if you feel you must go, but don't hurt my parents by keeping Rose from them or me." He closed the door and took off for the barn, leaving Iris to her turmoil.

CHAPTER NINETEEN

Caleb returned to the house later in the day to find Iris's car gone. He walked into the mudroom and put his coat on the peg, and kicked off his barn boots on the mat provided for them.

The kitchen door was closed to keep out the cold, and he stood there with his hand on the knob. Fortifying himself with a deep breath, he opened the door and stepped inside. He expected to find his parents sad as they sat at the supper table.

What he found was different from his imagination. Rose sat at her place at the table and welcomed him with a big, "*Gut daag, daed*."

"Hello back to you, *dochder*," he responded in kind.

Frowning, he looked around the room and didn't see Iris. So, she left. For some reason, when he saw Rose still here, he hoped she'd taken the car to the front of the house and parked there and entered the front door.

"She went back to the city, son. She asked us to keep Rose with us for a little while more until she could get her life sorted out." Daed said softly.

Caleb nodded and sat by Rose to join the family in prayer before they enjoyed supper.

Iris drove a few miles from Paradise Wells, and a horrible shaking overtook her body. She pulled into the first travel center she saw. After filling a plastic, insulated mug with strong coffee, she sat in the car drinking it.

Gott, please help me. I don't know what to do with my life. What is best for Rose? And for me? Only you can point me in the right direction. I give my life over to you. As you can see, I've made a mess of it so far without trusting you with the answers.

Then God spoke to her, bringing a Bible verse she had learned many years ago. *The heart of man plans his way, but the Lord establishes his steps.*

She put her mug in the console holder, started the car, and drove back onto the Interstate. His words had given her the direction she needed, and now, she knew what she had to do.

The drive back to the city wasn't as tricky as driving to Paradise Wells. She was sure now, and nothing would change her mind.

CHAPTER TWENTY

Three weeks later...

Caleb drove the wagon into Paradise Wells to pick up a special white oak order at the lumber yard. He planned to make a unique bedroom set for Rose. Dark wood wouldn't suit her, but a soft coloring would soothe her to sleep each night.

They hadn't heard a word from Iris. He ventured to think she was busy with her new job for doctor Rimmell in the city. Little Rose was busy with schoolwork he had set up with the local teacher for their district, Lillianna Beck. Each day, the teacher brought Rose's assignments and stayed for *kaffe* while explaining his daughter's work. Rose was advanced in her education which pleased him. He worried that her illness would have held her back. He could thank Iris for keeping Rose up to date with her schoolwork.

Just the thoughts of Iris pulled at his heart. He missed her. Each week he looked forward to seeing her arrive for her days off work.

As he entered the town, he spotted a moving van parked out in the street and saw a man using a cart tote in a stack of boxes into a large, vacant building next to the bakery. Daed spoke of some activity going on there because their storefront was on the other side of the bakery. He hadn't elaborated on it.

Caleb pulled the wagon around the back of the storefront and went inside to see his *daed*. He wanted to find out what sort of business was going into the building next door. Hopefully, not competition.

Suddenly, Caleb stopped dead in his tracts. Sitting with his father was Iris. His Iris, dressed in a blue Amish dress with a pristine white apron and on her head covering her red curls, was a *kapp*.

"Iris?"

Both David and Iris snapped their gazes in Caleb's direction.

Stepping through the showroom, he walked toward Iris. He couldn't look away. Why was she here? Why was she dressed in the customary Amish manner? Confusion swirled through him.

"I'll leave you two to talk. I'm going to the coffee shop for a nice caramel Macchiato."

Iris smiled at him and patted his hand.

David hurriedly left the store, leaving him and Iris alone.

"Iris? What is this all about?"

She stood and stepped the distance between them. Smiling, she offered. "I made my decision. I took doctor Stolfuz's offer, and he bought this building and is paying for the upgrades. We have modern equipment and technology here. And the Bishop approves!"

Caleb was stunned. "What does that mean for us? Are you telling me...?"

"I'm telling you that after a proper courtship, I'll marry you."

Reaching out, he wrapped his arms around Iris and pulled her to him.

"I love you, Caleb."

"I love you, too. I have forever. Please, let's sit. I need to know how all this happened. Why didn't you tell me you were coming home? Where will you live?"

Iris pulled him toward the chair where his father had been sitting. "Come here, and I'll explain."

Iris took a big breath and looked at him. He could see the love in her eyes, eyes so much like his daughter's.

"I started back to Lancaster, but deep in my heart, I knew I wanted to stay here with you and Rose. When I got the chance, I turned off the Interstate and drove a few miles back and went to see the doctor, and I accepted his offer. He planned on buying a vacant building on main street and had everything ordered or arranged for."

Caleb shook his head. "What if you'd told him, no?"

Iris laughed lightly. "I asked him that question myself. He told me, to get someone to take over the practice, he would have to make it possible with the new office. We talked at length about the practice, his role in it, and at the end, I knew I made the right decision."

"Why didn't you come and tell me? Do you know how upset I've been not hearing from you?"

Iris frowned. "I understand, but you have to remember, I wanted to do this on my own. I didn't need you running interference for me. Suppose I'm to be a strong, independent Amish doctor. In that case, I need the district and the Paradise Wells community to see me as such. I'm sorry if my absence hurt you. I had to do it my way.

Caleb nodded. He understood her actions. The Amish community wasn't accustomed to strong women, but when it came time for her to take care of men, she would need to show that power for them to accept her.

"Will you come live with us at the farm?"

Iris shook her head in answer. "No. The men are moving my belongings right now into the two-bedroom apartment over the medical office. Caleb, there is even a barn and a paddock for a horse behind the office!"

Taking her hand in his, he asked, "Will you please let me buy you a horse and covered buggy?"

Iris laughed. "I think I can accept that offer. I can't be traveling about in my car. Which, by the way, I sold."

Two hours later, Caleb drove the wagon, with Iris by his side, back to the farm. They just left the King farm, where they told her family the good news. Everyone hugged Iris, and tears flowed as they welcomed her home.

Now to tell Rose and his parents that Iris would be joining them for a future together in Paradise Wells.

THE END

Also by Piper Forrest

Quilted Hills

In Plain Sight

Amish Heritage

One Amish Autumn

My Amish Rose

Amish At Heart

Also by Lily Simmons

Quilted Hills

In Plain Sight

Amish Heritage

One Amish Autumn

My Amish Rose

Amish At Heart

www.ingramcontent.com/pod-product-compliance
Ingram Content Group UK Ltd.
Pitfield, Milton Keynes, MK11 3LW, UK
UKHW041822200726
13854UKWH00002BA/508